PRAISE FOR A~

Dig ᴍᴇ ᴏᴜ

"When I first encountered Amy Lillard's fiction in *Epiphany*'s Breakout Writers issue, I looked her up, desperately hoping she had a book coming out. The wait is over, and what a dazzling book it is! With spare and unassuming prose, Lillard has produced a radically profound and unforgettable story collection that up-ends received notions of femininity and storytelling. Through their aspirations, their desires, their insecurities, and their heartbreaks, the women in *Dig Me Out* offer us nuanced insights into the human condition."
—JEANNIE VANASCO, author of *Things We Didn't Talk About When I Was a Girl*

"Damn! I'm jealous of the sheer brio and adventure-someness of these stories — Amy Lee Lillard's willingness to try on different forms, genders, identities, and voices in the service of dark truths. This is a firecracker debut with a rock n roll wildness at its heart." —KARAN MAHAJAN, author of *The Association of Small Bombs*, National Book Award Finalist

"The women in these stories loom large. They take up space, raise their voice, fight back and break free. In stories spanning worlds long past to far dystopian future, we find women who channel rage and turn it into power, digging out of old lives, shedding skin, becoming something animal, elemental, new. These are queer women, but not just in sexuality: theirs are bodies in protest, retaliating against and reclaiming themselves from the patriarchal powers that attempt to own them, redefining what it means to be women, Set to a rebellious Riot Grrrl soundtrack, this book is a feminist battle cry, a fist with black-painted nails pumped in dark Chicago clubs, in Midwestern cities and suburbs full of women who are hungry, who long for more, who scratch and claw and dig — into the earth, into their own skin — to find something better. A fierce reclamation of femininity, sexuality, and selfhood, *Dig Me Out* made me pump my own fist in the air, reminding me of all the lives we can find when we're brave enough to dig." —MELISSA FALIVENO, author of *Tomboyland*

"Original and highly imaginative. Amy Lee Lillard is a daring writer." —CARTER SICKELS, author of *The Prettiest Star*

"A fierce debut collection inhabited by a wild multitude of characters. The women in Amy Lee Lillard's stories catalogue the strangeness of the natural world, want to escape the confines of the body, seek revenge against convention, are witchy, feral, ready to tear free."
—CHANELLE BENZ, author of *The Gone Dead*

"Buckle your belts — this rocket is ready to launch, and Saturnalia never felt so near!" —ROBERT ANTONI, author of *Cut Guavas* and *As Flies to Whatless Boys*

Amy Lee Lillard

DIG ME OUT

Amy Lee Lillard has been shortlisted for the Berlin Writing Prize and named one of *Epiphany's* Breakout 8 Writers. Her writing has appeared in *Barrelhouse, Foglifter, Off Assignment, Adroit, Gertrude,* and other publications. Lillard is one of the broads behind *Broads and Books,* a funny and feminist book podcast. She holds an MFA in fiction from the Pan-European MFA Program at Cedar Crest College, an MA in literature from Northwestern University, and a BA in English, journalism, and psychology from the University of Iowa.

AmyLeeLillard.com

DIG
ME
OUT

STORIES

Amy Lee Lillard

ATELIER26 BOOKS
Portland, OR

Dig Me Out (Fiction)
isbn-13: 978-1-7329896-6-5

Library of Congress Control Number: 2021943832

Atelier26 Books are printed in the U.S.A. on acid-free paper.

Cover illustration by Nathan Shields
Interior design by M.A.C.

ATELIER26 BOOKS, an independent press in
Portland, OR, exists to demonstrate the
powers and possibilities of literature through
beautifully designed and expressive books
that get people listening, talking, and
exchanging ideas. Our books have been
honored by the PEN/Hemingway Award,
the PEN/Robert W. Bingham Prize, the Balcones Fiction Prize,
and the Flann O'Brien Award, and cited on numerous Best of
the Year lists.

The valued support of Jason Headley and Literary Arts helped
make this book possible.

Atelier26Books.com

For the women who won't smile

CONTENTS

DIG ME OUT

BANG BANG

RIGHT AFTER MOM FINISHES THE STORY OF LOSING HER virginity to Dad, we hit the animal. We're going sixty-seven on two-lane asphalt in our brand new 1989 Riviera, so we don't see the thing in time. The FM radio is cutting out in that no-man's-land between counties, but we hear Cher belt out her wish to turn back time right as we feel the impact and hear a crunch. One of the tires loses grip of the road, so for a second we're on three wheels, and from the floor the McDonalds bag and fry wrappers kick up to my seat, and the Diet Cokes tilt in their cup holders and leak brown sugar water on the leather dash. Mom stomps both pointed mules against the car's carpet and we skid and shake and stop.

This happens when I'm almost twelve. Later, when I'm thirty-eight, it happens again.

I'm driving on a suburban side street, all grown up in my brand new 2015 Prius. In its dash is a computer screen that would look like sci-fi to my adolescent self. Music plays from my phone through the car speakers, Nancy Sinatra singing about her baby that shot her down. I'm going the speed limit of thirty-five. I'm thinking about the stranger I met on an app, his quick, soulless, mechanical thrusting twenty minutes ago, this man who paid little attention to my body other than to stick himself into it. That's when I hit the animal. Bang bang, Nancy says. A bump, like driving over a curb, and my phone falls under the plastic dash. I yelp and slam on the brakes.

"Grandma never talked to me about sex," Mom had said. "Or losing her virginity, or what boys were like. I want to be different. I want you to know what to expect."

Jesus Christ, my mother says when I'm twelve.

Fuck me, I say when I'm thirty-eight.

In the Riviera, Mom's arms are twitching, bare and mottled with moles. We've stopped in the middle of the highway, Mom breathing hard and snotting up, so I remind her we need to pull to the gravel shoulder. I check the back seat, my nine-year-old brother still asleep, mouth open and tongue out, a comic book shot of a dead villain. Mom reaches to the gearshift on the wheel, and her hand is shaking so bad all her charm bracelets and bangles make a tambourine sound.

I'm thirty-eight and I'm shaking too, my leather cuff rapping against my wrist and ergonomic wheel. I ease the Prius onto the paved shoulder. I really need to pee.

> "I was fourteen.
> Your dad was
> sixteen. He'd had
> sex before. He
> wanted sex
> again."

I don't want to see, Mom says when we've stopped and she's shifted to park. We don't have to, I say. At this age I still think of most animals in a cartoon setting. Only once every few months do we get out in the country like this. Dirt-yellow cornfields, small brown dots that are real horses and cows. Metal-gray roads, brownish-blue skies. *To grandmother's house we go.* Back home where it's concrete and exhaust and sirens the only animal I see is our fat housecat who poops in a box — and the anemic birds that perch on our wooden deck railing. I'm not sure I want to see a bigger animal, especially if it's bloody.

Thirty-eight, and I still don't want to see. Animals are pure. They don't deserve pain, and blood, from some dumbass distracted driver like me.

> "I asked your
> grandma about
> sex. She didn't

answer at first.
But eventually she
admitted she'd
had sex at
thirteen. It was
past time for me,
she said."

We need to make sure it's dead, Mom says, the last word spread over five or six wailing syllables. I ask her what she'll do if it's not dead. I don't know, she says, head in hands. I look at her jewelry, makeup, clothes. So much lacquer and lace. She encourages me to do the same, to make an effort. But I look at my dad, how he doesn't have to put shit on his face or jewels on his fingers to leave the house. Maybe men, free of that stuff, have more space to be strong. I think about what Dad would do if he were here, dig out a crowbar or a hammer from the trunk and bash the animal's skull in. Or maybe he'd have a gun stowed in the glove. He's pretty decisive that way. But these trips are for us alone, Mom says. We're not supposed to ask what Dad does on his free weekends away, or whether my brother and I can also take a pass and stay home.

When I'm thirty-eight, looking down on my parents for all their failings, real and imagined, thinking about my Mom and Dad as humans rather than looming presences, considering how they're a generation that needs to cede the floor, their all-caps email forwards about women kidnapped by sex traffickers in mall

16

bathrooms and their loud praying at restaurants before meals, I wish Dad were here, but I know I have to take care of my own goddamn mess.

> "I kept him
> wanting. It was a
> game. Offense vs
> defense. Like
> football. Your dad
> was so good at
> football, and I
> cheered at his
> football games. So
> I knew the rules."

Mom had been talking about animals before we hit one. Men are the wolves, she'd said. We're the deer. I sort of get it, even if we don't see a lot of wolves or deer at home. At school, I've already been hearing about kids in my grade fucking in their above-ground pools (super-hot, they say), and one girl who let a guy stick his penis in her ass (he pulled out and it was brown, they say) and one girl who let a guy eat her out when she was on her period (he got his redwings, they say). That's the talk in the halls. The boys in detention, in the room adjoining where I tutor one of the pregnant girls, they say even more, and they look at us and waggle their tongues between V'd fingers. Our school is made of the kids of plumbers and electricians, bank tellers and cops, grocery baggers and day care workers.

In these two rooms after school the future rapists and meth heads mix with the pregnant teens and the scared geeks.

At thirty-eight, Mom's words are in my head, from that day and many after. Boys like the hunt.

Did we hit a deer? asks my brother from the backseat, rubbing his ears. Go back to sleep, Mom says. It's louder than it needs to be, and has that snarly tone to it, so my brother lies back down. Fast as Mom's tears can come, she can also switch to yelling. That's always there, the ready anger when we track mud on the carpet, when I shrug at a shirt she holds up for my approval three aisles away at Kmart, when my brother swings too slow and strikes out.

At thirty-eight, I've always thought I skipped that loud anger, that rawness. Usually I keep quiet until my anger eats away at my stomach and esophagus and bowels. Later I'll have diarrhea, and maybe chest pain that the internet tells me might be a heart attack or maybe *just* a panic attack. Usually, to stay calm, I breathe from my gut like my therapist says. I've never yelled and screamed and cried. Until tonight, anyway.

"Boys like games, sweetheart. They especially like games they can win."

In the Riviera, I open the car door, push it with my

leg because it's so heavy. I'm tall, already at my full height of five foot eleven, towering over most others in my class. I'm tall and I'm technically a woman because my periods started when I was ten. Mom gave me this half-smile when I told her, handed me tampons I didn't know how to use, shut me in the bathroom. She's never had many women friends, so from the time I came out of the bathroom our conversations changed. On these trips into the countryside she tells me how unfair her boss is, how little she makes, how Dad won't take her anywhere and how she regrets her choices in life. I get a heavy feeling each time we take these drives, knowing the complaints she's going to unload on me.

At thirty-eight, unmarried and childless in my space-age Prius, I think how no one but me will have to bear this burden.

"Boys like a hunt."

I step out of the car, when I'm twelve and when I'm thirty-eight. I look behind, the way I came, toward the dead thing. It's sunny when I'm young, midnight dark when I'm old. A biting autumn wind blows both times. The shoulder is gravel when Mom yells at me to wait, and paved when I hear nothing. The thing on the ground twitches, and my hips too, shaking knees and full bladder.

"Boys like to show
how strong they

19

are, show how
weak everyone
else is."

In the sunlight I see a blood trail leading to the shape on the gravel. It's dark and muddy, the same color as my period blood. Shocking, the idea of that bright red liquid pouring from the spigot of my body. That's what I'd imagined after the Home Ec teacher in fourth grade told us about the changes we could expect. That's what I'd imagined after seeing *Carrie*. Instead it was just my underpants smudged brown, and I wondered if I was somehow different than the other girls. Did they get the periods you learned about from stories and movies? Were they more woman than me? Maybe that's who Mom wants me to be.

In the moonlight I can't see the animal's blood, but I smell rust and something rotting, the stink of micro-waved broccoli in a tight company kitchen. Something human too, familiar from decades of grappling with other bodies in beds, in cars, against walls. Their sweat, their semen.

"He hunted me,
and he got me."

Mom yells at me to get back in the car, but I keep following the trail until my knock-off blue Keds almost touch the animal. It's oblong and fat, and it's black with bits of white, and finally my brain puts it together and names the shape *raccoon*. The fur on its side is matted, and its chest goes up and down, up and down, in a broken way, and there's a gurgling groan from its throat. I look back at the Riviera, Mom's head poking out the window. She's gesturing, quick swipes, gold rings catching the sunlight. Dad gives her one every Christmas for another year of peace, but nowadays they only buy him a few weeks. At twelve I still believe in God, and now Mom's rings shoot rays that look like some sort of sign. *Honor thy father and mother.* And maybe it's now that I start to wonder about God and his rules.

In the dark, steps from my Prius, godless for years and years, I assess the shape on the asphalt. It's smaller than a raccoon, and I feel a punch in my throat when I realize it's a cat. Maybe a stray, the feral kind that hisses when you get too close. Or maybe a house tabby, escaped for a moment to hunt pests and huff the night air. I think of my indoor cat at home, that pleading look, how she begs me to let her follow her instincts and run the night. It feels a bit obscene, and definitely disrespectful of the dead, but I can't wait anymore. Lights are off in the house across the street, so I squat down behind a tree a few yards from the cat, kick off my heels and spread my toes in well-kept grass. I lift my skater skirt and piss. Convenient I skipped putting my underwear back on, the nice lacy ones he'd barely looked at in his haste to unwrap a condom. Sighing as my bladder lightens, I watch the cat's sides. They don't move.

"It hurt a lot. I
won't lie about
that. But he was
so happy. It felt
good to make him
happy."

The raccoon moves, though. It's twisting its neck and mewling, torn between keeping eyes on me and scrambling away. Mom screams not to touch it, to get back in the goddamn car. But I watch as the raccoon's motion slows, and at first I think it's recognized me, seen the kindness in my soul and knows me for one of the good humans. That's what I hope, but it's only a hope. Because then the raccoon isn't watching me at all. Its black eyes, wide and searching, are fixed on the sky. I imagine it's trying to remember who it is, where it is, what food tasted like, what air felt like, what this life was for. Its front paws widen, the digits and claws spreading, as if it wants to grab anything, everything. The raccoon's sides hitch and roll as it fights to breathe.

Done peeing now, I get close and crouch over the cat, whose eyes are open, slits of moonlit yellow just visible. It's definitely dead. I'm trying to sit with that a minute, acknowledge what I've done. But I'm craving a cigarette. I've cut way down. No more smoky bourbon and pack of American Spirits each weekend night. I used to smoke sometimes after sex. Watching '80s soft-core movies late at night as a teen taught me the two were paired. I always thought that would mark my arrival in adulthood for sure — lying next to a lover on creamy crisp white sheets, coverlet halfway up my breasts, the lover watching the cigarette burning between my scarlet-letter lips. When sex finally happened in college, the sheets were often gray and sticky. The man underneath me would pass out within minutes after he'd come, my body buzzing yet still wanting. I smoked then, rising up from my body with carbon-filled exhales. Nothing was quite as I pictured. But it did feel good, the smoking. It felt nice to die a little after feeling a bit more alive.

"That's what makes something last. If you care more about making someone else happy, no matter how it hurts."

You'll meet a boy in high school, Mom had said. You'll like him. He'll want things from you.

At both ages my hands are in front of me, moving toward the raccoon, toward the cat. I know this isn't wise — that dying and dead animals bring danger and disease — but I want to touch anyway. Eyes can only do so much. The raccoon stiffens. The cat is already stiff.

> "Girls lives are
> short, sweetheart.
> Sex is the end of
> girlhood."

I hear the Riviera door open behind me, wailing guitar escaping into the country air. My mother is out on the shoulder, mules pounding as she comes for me. My hand moves closer to the raccoon, and the raccoon watches me, and I think I recognize that look of giving up. I've seen it on adults. I look at the raccoon's shape and wonder what will happen to the body when it dies. There is no such thing as roasted raccoon, so will it just rot? It's the way things are, Mom and Dad say when I question why we eat cow and not cat. I can picture their revulsion if I were to ask about raccoon. There's a rule at play that says some animals are for eating and killing, and some for petting and cuddling. The ones we eat don't think like us, Mom and Dad say.

The cat is dead. I wonder if someday that kind of death will mean food for us. The world seems to be moving in weird directions, exploding in size and stupidity. So maybe that's how we'll solve the problem of feral felines running the towns. I'm thinking about what cat must taste like, and then I'm craving a cigarette even more.

> "Boys lives are
> long, though. Sex
> is just the start."

The raccoon seems to fade and go limp as my hand gets closer, and I hear my mother's feet on the gravel, and my pointer finger makes contact with rough bristly damp fur, and as it does the animal shudders. It sort of sags, and it looks like a stuffed toy my brother dragged up and down the stairs, squeezing until the stitching burst and oily gray cotton came out. My mother grabs my bicep and pulls and my feet slide out from under me. She's blocking the sun as I look up, her face shadowed. I don't need to see that look though, I've seen it plenty. When she heads back for the car, yelling that I better follow or she's leaving me here, I pull up my hand and it's got red smears dotted with black bits of ground asphalt. I'm pretty sure it's not my blood.

The boy you like, Mom had said. He'll want to have sex.

Meanwhile I'm reaching out my older, pale pointer finger toward the cat. I make contact with the back leg. It's so thin and small, and I could probably wrap my fist around it, apply a tiny bit of pressure, snap it. I wonder what that would sound like. A twig? The pop of my ankles as I descend stairs? A paintball gunshot? It wouldn't hurt her. Her, because I still default to cats as girls and dogs as boys. Wherever she is, this cat, it's not here. And the road crews, the parolees and high school dropouts who sweep the shoulders for dead deer and possums and squirrels, will probably mangle the cat's body far worse. It doesn't matter what I do, I think, as I press a little on the leg that feels like a turkey wishbone. I sometimes wish my cat would be as cold and rigid as this one. The act of taking care of her, of the small necessities of food each morning and night in her silver bowls, scooping her litter box for the clumps of shit, sweeping the stray bits of litter that follow her down the stairs, giving her the love and attention she craves. It's all so minor and easy, but it's often overwhelming.

> "Maybe it's not
> fair. That's what
> some women say.
> But it's life."

Back in the car with mom and my brother, we pull out a little too fast and the rear wheel drive makes us skid. I turn in my seat, look behind us, and the body of the raccoon gets smaller and smaller. I think of movies, women thrown in the backs of cars, holding their hands out against the rear window glass, crying for mercy. I want to hold my hand out like that.

After a few minutes of staring at the cat's body, I return to the Prius and grab a towel from the backseat. I lay it over and around the cat's body, then shift its weight to my arms. The trunk is full, and not for her. I put the dead body on my passenger seat.

> "Soon, you'll meet
> a boy. You'll like

him. He'll want
things from you."

We're quiet in the Riviera. My brother is pretending
to sleep in the back. My mother is curled over the
steering wheel, rigid and wary. I'm sneaking glances at
my red right hand. It's the hand I write with, tight little
scrawls on worksheets and in my diary. It's the hand I
wipe myself with, on the toilet and in the shower. It's
the hand I use when I'm exploring down there, probing
to see what my body is shaped like, pushing and
rubbing when something feels good. I expect the hand
to feel different, since I touched the raccoon at its
moment of death. I wonder if touching the raccoon
made it die. It makes this hand different from other
hands. From Mom's.

I start up my Prius and return to the road, carrying
the living and the dead.

"You'll never be as
happy as that first
time you're
chased. It's such a
wonderful feeling,
being wanted.
Even if it's only for
your body."

When Mom pulls the Riviera off the highway and
starts down the lane towards my grandmother's house,

my brother bolts upright in the back seat and Mom
puts a hand on my arm. She asks if I'm all right. I shrug
and there's a beat where I could say something, where I
could ask all the questions I have in my head, all the
why's. I rub at the fading red on my hand. The raccoon
probably had sex before it died. Everything and
everyone has sex. I will have sex someday, apparently
sooner than I thought. I think about my periods,
cramping guts and sore breasts. Is it painful like that?
What if he wants to have sex while I'm bleeding? What
if he makes me bleed?

I pull the Prius onto the highway, and drive away
from my house, away from the city lights into the dark.

"Keep him
wanting. Then you
can keep him.
Maybe even marry
him after high
school, and have
a family. Maybe
that can work for
you."

I swallow the questions I have for Mom, knowing
somehow the answers will only spark more. Then Mom
says she has something else to tell me.

Driving in my Prius, I think again about tonight's
sex. The vacant look on his face as he shoved his fingers
around in my vagina, then his dick. The look of nausea

on his face after a few thrusts. He'd pulled out and collapsed sideways on his king bed lit by the hall halogen. His wad blown, I was a human again, and worthy of his words. And he was full of them: tales of divorce, his first one and his second. Judgment of the girls on Tinder and their superficiality. The facts on how women have ruined his life. The air shifted then, in that way the females of the species are taught to notice.

"Be careful, though. Don't make him wait too long. Wolves can't control themselves after a while."

In the Riviera, Mom says she has a suitcase packed for me in the trunk. We're not going home at the end of the weekend. We're moving into Grandma's house for a while. We're doing this because she's leaving Dad.

Outside the city I pull the Prius onto a rural road of gravel and dust. After a couple miles I drive off the shoulder and into a black field lit only by a half-moon and billions of stars. I think of all the boys and men since that day in the Riviera.

"Don't make him wait too long. Better for him,

and better for you
to get it over
with."

In the Riviera, Mom tells me how it will be. Hard at first, but for the best. She pats my arm and gets out of the car to greet grandma. I think about how quick Mom switches from anger to tears. How both permeate every word.

Outside the Prius, I use the ice scraper as a makeshift shovel, slowly digging into the earth. As I dig I think of my meek men, my domesticated dogs. I'd avoided boys all through high school, afraid to get trapped before I was done being a girl. In college I spotted a shy boy in the corner at a party and I took him back to my dorm. Me on top, him pinned under my legs. I fucked others like him through college, quiet and unkempt, wiener dogs instead of wolves. Grateful for attention, they didn't mind when I took control, told them what to do. Different men over the years but the same man, same script: lick the penis and balls but never put them in my mouth. Lower myself over his face but never let him make me come. Let him fill me, let him grip me, let him moan and growl, but only from a prone position. I'm always in charge, never vulnerable. And I think of how I got bored, so bored I swiped right on someone neat, trimmed, muscled.

"So that's how the
world works,

30

sweetheart. I'm so
glad I told you, so
you know what to
expect. So much
better than
ignoring it, like my
mom. You're
lucky."

In the Riviera I sit long after Mom has gone inside
grandma's house. Our new home. I think of Dad,
washing his car when we left. In my memory I make
him look at me, let me examine his eyes and face and
lips to see if I can spot the snout and canines and slits of
pupils. But I just see a man, unaware of this cleaving
moment, this catastrophic loss of the game.

Outside the Prius I place the dead cat into the small
hole I've dug and replace the dirt. I stand over her for a
moment. No god, but something animal, natural, feels
right with this act. Then I open my trunk. The shape
within shifts. He'd been brief, and rude, and clueless,
and that was all fine. But then, engorged by his tales of
demonic women, he'd pushed me back on the bed. And
when he pinned my arms above my head I thought of
being hunted, torn apart, and hung up on a wall as a
prize. I got loose from his grip, and without thought,
pure animal instinct, grabbed the heaviest thing nearby,
the bedside table lamp, and smashed it over his head.

"These? I'm just
crying because I'm
happy. All our
emotions are
mixed together,
you know. We
can't separate
being sad and
being happy. Or
even being mad!
It's what makes
us females."

The sun is setting. So I leave the Riviera and start
my future.

In the field, my trunk open. The man who thought
he was a wolf lies curled up inside. Bleeding, bound and
taped, but still alive. Mine to control. His eyes are open
in half-slits, and I cock my finger and thumb like a gun.
Bang bang, I say, and close the trunk.

HEAD LIKE A HOLE

I FOUND A HOLE WHEN I WAS WEEDING, I SAID.

We were in bed, our backs against the headboards. He had his latest ra-ra-team-building book open in his lap, his reading glasses on.

In the front yard, I said. Between the smoke tree and the hostas.

He used to be the chatty one at night, ready to talk about minutiae and mindworms, pulling me away from the gory and gruesome pages in my own lap.

It's precise too, I said. Six inches deep. A couple inches across.

He looked at me then, his eyes magnified to comic ovals. That's great babe, he said. What're you going to put there?

I'm not planting anything, I said. The hole was just there.

He glanced down. The tear in my Sonic Youth t-shirt showed a stripe of flesh near my nipple.

Oh, he said. You think we have chipmunks, or moles, or something?

The lettering on his Blackhawks t-shirt was nearly gone.

No, I said. Not their type of hole.

Hmm, he said. He put his book down and shifted his body towards me. He threw out more ideas: mountain lions, coyotes. Nothing he'd ever seen in our town, he said, but the expanding boundary lines of Chicago suburbs might confuse wild animals. Trap them in a quiet street like ours.

I watched him talk himself further from reality, noted the patches of skull showing through brown and gray hairs, the blooming belly and budding breasts. Fat replacing muscle, hair migrating across his body, things reversing themselves. And in response to that movement, I saw only peace and contentment.

He fell asleep mid-sentence, his words transforming to nonsense sounds. Then, that familiar soft snore, the one that sounded like he was snuffling through silt.

*

Animals that dig holes: moles. Chipmunks. Skunks. Groundhogs. They dig out grubs and earthworms for meals, seeds and bulbs for snacks. They build burrows and tunnels for shelter. Wild things are living in this sedate suburb. Underneath us.

When I can't sleep, and I can never sleep, I study holes and their makers. I scour the web for pictures, the unique identifiers of each hole to each species. I take notes.

This is not crazy. This is what forty-nine-year-old women do. We throw ourselves into gardening, and we knead all we can out of our plot of earth. We buy gloves and hats, trowels and shovels. We grip green things and we decide what lives and dies. We nurture and grow. We watch things transform.

*

This is crazy, I said the next night. I stood in our bedroom, in my cargo pants and Replacements t-shirt, sweat in the pits and grass on the knees. The hole is bigger, I said.

You're tracking mud, he said from the bed. I pictured all the ants and mites and tiny spiders and fleas that might have hitched a ride indoors on me.

I measured it, I said. It's definitely bigger.

You measured it?

Come see!

He pointed to his book, something ra-ra-team-engagement. His GenX mindset was outdated, the new VP at his work had said. He needed to better speak to Millennials, the VP said, and assigned a syllabus of modern corporate bibles.

Did you cut yourself?

I looked at where he pointed, the crook of my left arm. I didn't see anything.

Come on, I said, and ran to the front door.

When he joined me, he had a Band-Aid in his hand. Let me help, he said.

See? I said. It's out there, and I pointed through the screen.

Your hostas look great, babe, but—

I switched on the patio light, pushed through the storm door, and slipped into my outdoors shoes. He called after me, and I gestured for him to follow.

We stood at the hole.

Maybe... he said.

I watched his lips move as his brain worked.

Don't they have a Lab? He pointed towards the red Victorian, three houses down from our Craftsman.

It's not a dog, I said. Look. He followed my index finger. It's ten inches across now, I said. A foot deep.

He stood with his hands on his hips, a picture of superhero concentration. A forty-nine-year-old man. I'm sure that's what he was thinking. A homeowner, a people manager, a husband of two decades. A knower of things, a problem solver. He probably thought I was looking to him for answers.

I felt a tenderness towards him then, that soft ache of a bruise in my chest. And I thought of just filling that hole in, the two of us. The hole could be something we wondered at, laughed at, something new to share.

But then he shrugged, his shoulders hitching sharply. I'll fill it in tomorrow, he said.

No, I said too loud. It's there for a reason.

What's the reason?

I felt my own sharpness, a whip of anger. Don't you want to find out?

*

Animals that shed skin: snakes. Lizards. Salamanders. Frogs. Hermit Crabs. Some of them eat the skin once it's shed.

At night, when I can't sleep, and I can never sleep, I take long showers. I scrub, sloughing off dead skin cells on my loofah, and I shave, stripping my legs and crotch and belly and nipples and underarms of hair. After toweling off I scrape my feet with an emery board, bits of the callouses on my toes and heels coming away like coconut flakes. I sniff at them, dip my tongue into the pile and taste absence.

This is not crazy. This is what all animals do. We molt, and sometimes we consume ourselves for nutrients. We change. We transform in the ways available to us.

*

This is crazy, I said, but I want you to keep watch with me.

He looked at me a long time, and I could catalogue what he saw. The lost elasticity of my breasts, hanging down like pendants. The slackness of my stomach, gut bulging my stretched-out t-shirt. The missing color and life of my hair, long and limp against my neck. Like him, I was slowly sinking, gravity pulling at every part of us.

OK, he said. But doesn't it feel like we're spying on our neighbors?

I pulled him into the living room, onto the brown microfiber loveseat from Room and Board. I turned the lights out.

He shrugged and sank down, smiling at the new game.

He talked at first, about the VP, the books he'd been assigned on management and personality scoring and conflict resolution. He wondered if the VP was trying to retrain him, or push him out. He asked about my current contract, UX design for an agency in the city. He asked about the people he knew. I answered in hmms and ohs and fines.

He asked how late we were going to stay up.

Until we see what's happening, I said.

You get a scrape again?

I followed his finger to my knee. I didn't see anything.

Watch, I said, pointing outside.

We sat in the dark and waited. The clock on the living room wall circled past eleven, then midnight. I felt him shifting more, jolting himself awake.

Remember when we'd just be getting started around this time? He scratched at his throat and shook his head. Hammering down shots over your sink, then cabbing to Neo? Thrashing all night? Then...

I drummed my fingers on the couch and remembered the harsh house lights coming on at five AM, sending all the night's children scurrying. We'd make our way home, feet throbbing from the concrete dance floor, heads pounding with the echo of punk and goth beats.

I'd turn rabid when we got back to my loft. Command him: fill me, bite me, tear me apart. And he'd obey.

Around one in the morning, he whispered, what are you expecting to see?

I'm not expecting anything, I said.

What if it's a neighbor?

It's not a neighbor, I said.

But what if...

He fell asleep mid-sentence, slumping down in his seat.

*

Animals that morph: the mutable rain frog. The golden tortoise beetle. The cuttlefish. The mimic octopus. Most change their skin and coloring for defense, or as a surprising offense.

At night, when I can't sleep, and I can never sleep, I try on wigs. I paint my face. I dig out old clothes I never gave away.

When he and I were young, dancing till five, I did this for real. I dyed my hair jet black, wore leather and black lips. I cut and spiked my hair with fuchsia, wore babydoll dresses and combat boots. I slicked my hair back, wore suspenders and a bow tie, handkerchief in my jeans pocket. I changed my body, and my body became change.

At some point, the only change left was age. Do the things older women did. Trade in discount paint brushes and kitchen shears for a stylist's chair and foil,

Wicker Park for Wilmette. Leave behind Riot Grrrl; embrace gardening. I was to watch things transform under my tutelage, and be comfortable with constancy.

This is not crazy. It's what animals do.

*

This is crazy, I said the next morning. But it's bigger. So we need to watch again.

Still in the loveseat, he stretched his arms overhead, the picture of rest. We need sleep, he said.

You got sleep.

Babe, he said, rubbing at the steel wool on his cheeks. We can't do all-nighters anymore.

I wanted to tell him that all my nights were all-nighters.

I'm staying up, I said. I want you to join me.

OK, he said, his eyes wide. I never made demands.

So that night, after his shower, and the next night, and the night after that, I led him into the living room. We turned off the lights, settled into the couch. I watched the lawn. He watched me.

Remember, he'd say. The quiet and the dark now made him nostalgic. He became the chatty one again. Remember the song you danced to at Neo?

The DJ played Bauhaus, Ministry, Depeche Mode, and I danced to all of it. I was twenty with a fake ID and black eyes, and the bouncer let me in every time. The dance floor spun and cratered, smoke silhouetting all of us. One night they played a new song with heavy synths and pounding drums. Head like a hole, black as your soul. I thrashed, kicked, headbanged, jumped. My hair long and black, a whip I wielded.

Remember, he said, laughing a little. The alley?

When the bar closed, he followed me into the long alley to the street. I pulled him out of the exodus and up against the brick wall. The words I said lost to the ringing in both of our ears, to the thrum of blood as I pulled him into a cab.

Remember, he said, looking at my Bikini Kill t-shirt with pit stains. All the shirts you stole?

We'd go to cheap shows, the bands playing small clubs before grunge and punk went mainstream. Some bands got bigger, some died after the show. He distracted the merch guys with questions about stickers and buttons, and I'd lift what I could, slip off through the crowd. Back in my loft, he called me sneaky and wild, grew hard. I made noises, guttural and gritty.

After, when he slept, I'd unroll the t-shirts, smooth them out. I'd feel a part of something.

Remember, he said, pulling me back to then, ignoring now.

He fell asleep mid-memory.

*

Animals that age: all of them.

At night, I count all the Me's. Purple-haired, brunette, black, bleached blonde. Cigarette-thin and healthy-fat. New Wave, Goth, Punk. Anti-marriage,

wife. Feminist, realist. Transforming my shape, my
outlook, my Me-ness, searching for the thing that
would snap into place and make this carcass feel like
home.

But it never worked. And now the carcass is hard-
ening, calcifying with age.

I have to cut it back, force myself out, do what
animals do.

This isn't crazy. This is crazy. This isn't crazy. This
is—

*

What are you doing?

I froze, my hands curled around dirt. The man
behind me.

Hey, he said. What are you doing?

I sniffed, smelled his swamp breath and sweat. I
turned around in the hole, which now came to my waist,
breathing hard, exhaling little grunts. I saw what he
saw, the dirt on my feet and hands, my threadbare Nine
Inch Nails t-shirt. Digging, hunched over, dirt flying
between my legs to arc into the air.

I woke up, he said, and you weren't there.

He'd hoped for something small. I know he'd imagined running out of the house, waving his arms wildly
at the animal at fault, baring his chest and bleating in
the language of animal alphas.

Every night? He was shrinking before me, cowering.
Or I was growing taller.

I brought my fingers to my face and striped my cheeks with dirt.

I don't understand, he said.

My throat only grunted and growled. Animals don't use words. They dig. They run. They tear and bite and gnash teeth.

Hey, he said, and I could hear the plea there. Talk to me.

I took a deep breath of the night air, felt the wind pull and curl my hair into a crown. Then I crawled from the hole and loped towards the house, my limbs loose and hot.

Wait, he said.

The door was open, an overconfident male leaving his burrow unguarded.

You can tell me, he said, please, tell me, what's happening, what what what

My feet trailed dirt on the stairs, leaving tracks another animal could find. So I made for the bathroom, stripped off my t-shirt and underwear, turned on the tap.

He gasped. What happened?

I looked down at my naked body. I saw rotting meat, like always.

He touched my arm, and I bared my teeth. Babe, seriously, what is this? He pointed.

I looked again. My breasts were dotted with dirt and cuts like extra nipples. My stomach was red with scabs and raw skin. My pubic hair had gone patchy, my legs bore razor nicks in the shape of stripes. Everywhere, small ovals of skin missing, some oozing.

The man breathed horror in and out. I remembered it'd been a long time since he'd seen me naked. I remembered how low and driving the drumbeat in that song, how hard I pounded the floor with my feet.

I raked my nails across my breasts, creating red welts. I need out, I said.

Stop, he said.

This is dead, I said, drawing over the lines again with my nails. Blood seeped from one path.

Stop!

He looked at me, and I know he was searching for that young girl pounding the concrete, black boots and black shirts and black hair, combat gear for war on the dance floor.

She's in here, I said. She's trapped.

Babe, what are you talking about? What did you do?

I can't be this anymore, I said. This skin. It's not me. I grabbed at my breasts, pulled at them hard. This isn't me, I said.

You mean, he said. I watched him stall, watched him struggle. I watched him, and I wanted him to understand. I felt that tenderness again, that bruise. He could help if I let him, if I—

Are you, do you think you're, depressed? His mouth curled around the words he never used. Or maybe, he said. Could it be, pre-menopausal?

I'm buried alive, I said, and the heat tore through my throat into a nonsense sound, a growl and a groan.

The water still ran, and the steam rose. I stepped

into the shower, and watched my dirt gather at the drain. My skin turned brown and slid down into a pool of rust.

He leaned against the sink, making sounds that were probably words. Asking questions: was the job the problem? The house? The move out of the city? Or the things we hadn't done, the traveling, the procreating? Or was it the distance between us, the nights in bed with books and not each other. Or, he mused, let's face it, we were getting older, right, and we were starting to sag and shrink in weird places. Our bodies would no longer let us dance all night and tear each other apart. And that's tough, he admitted, and maybe we need to talk about that, maybe with someone else.

Why, I said.

What?

Why didn't you know, I said. That it was me?

You mean — digging the hole?

You don't see me, I said.

That's not, that's not right.

Because this isn't me, I said.

Wait, he said, waving his arms. Wait. Why did you do this? Did you trick me? You, you set a trap is what you did. Why?

I thought of animals that set traps. Stoats pretend to convulse to draw bunnies closer for the kill. Jaguars and pumas mimic primates to bring them near. And the Amazonian spider makes a massive facsimile of itself with debris and web, to ward off predators. This is something animals do.

At my silence, my distance, he stripped down, pulled off his Bears t-shirt and gym shorts, his loose plaid boxers and watch. He shivered when he stepped into the shower.

We faced each other.

Please babe, he said. Tell me what to do.

He was always good at this, at following my lead.

I see you, he said. For, what, all these years. I see you. I love you.

I watched his mouth move. His words pinged off my skin like hail.

What do you see, I said.

He smiled. How you dance, he said. How you move. No one and nothing moves like you.

I don't feel this body, I said. I don't feel it move.

That's not true, he said, grabbing my shoulders, shaking me a little. You used to snarl and bite at me in bed. Remember? That loft mattress. You'd rip through me to get to me. And then you'd just give yourself over. The way you shook, the sounds you made. Fuck, I'd lose it just watching you.

That was— I stopped. Was she buried in here? Did she ever really exist?

He reached behind me and turned the now-cold water off. He pulled the towel from the rack, draped it over my shoulders.

We're older, he said. We're different. That's all true. And I look at myself and wonder who that is. I do. Jesus. It's like, it's like opposite day or something. My hair, my gut. And when I think about it too much, it makes me, god, almost crazy.

This isn't crazy, I said.

No, I know.

This is crazy, I said. The two of us. We don't belong out here.

He laughed. But you wanted to move out here! You said you wanted this.

I wanted to be something else, I said.

Shit, babe, that's easy. Remember how much you used to change? Do it again. Try something new.

I did, I said, pointing out the door.

I can join you, he said. I'll go to the gym. I'll, fuck it, I'll get a new job. I'll make more time for you. We can do this together. We can go to counseling even. We can make a change.

I did, I said again.

What do you mean?

I dug.

He squinted at me.

I tried to do the things I could, I said. I planted hostas. I pruned the trees. I weeded. I—

The towel fell off my shoulders as I felt a growl escape my throat.

I found holes, I said. So I researched what they could be. And I found all these things animals do. The ways they change to survive.

He trembled, and tried not to.

I'm just an animal, I said.

OK, he said to the floor of the tub.

But I can't morph anymore, or shed my skin. Not

fully. I don't get to.

OK. He stepped out, wrapped my discarded towel around his waist.

But I can dig a hole.

OK. OK. He did that thing where he bounced on his toes a bit. OK, he said again. I've got an idea.

He grabbed my hand, pulled, and I let him. He jogged, leading my naked body behind him out of the bathroom, down the dirt-covered stairs, into the dark living room. He dropped my hand, then powered up the turntable and speakers. He found the record, put the needle in the right groove.

Watching me, he bobbed his head to the first snare hits and the wordless cries. Then, banged his head to the keyboards and guitar.

I looked out the window, at the hole.

Dance, babe, he said over the dark beat. You remember.

His bare feet began to pound the carpet in a sort of march and jump. The towel fell away, and he was a middle-aged man with paunch and thick pubic hair, his face turning red. He sang along with Trent Reznor, and his throat turned into thick cords of effort.

Dance!

The chorus started, and his muscle memory took over, pogoing up and down, pumping his arms, sweat beading along his forehead and neck.

He stopped as the chorus went back to verse.

Come on, babe, he said, huffing.

I shook my head.

Dance with me. You can do this.

I shook my body, darted between him and the record player.

Stop, he said, as I reached for the stylus. He grabbed my arm, pulled me toward him, and I yanked away, back to the record player. He grabbed me again, and I yanked again. He grabbed both arms, and I pushed him, and he stumbled, turned his ankle, swore.

I ran, out the front door that still stood open to the night.

At the lip of the hole, I looked down. At night, when I couldn't sleep, and I could never sleep, not in this town with the quiet of a tomb, I came out here and I dug. First with the tools afforded women who garden. Then with feet, kicking away clods of dirt and stamping down what remained. Then, with hands, claws, my entire body burrowing into the earth to find what hid underneath.

This isn't crazy, I said when I heard him behind me again.

I didn't say that, he said, his voice high and tight, his body still naked.

Through the open door, the song, the drums.

When my hands and claws gave out, I'd brought out my exacto knife, the one he used to slice open boxes in the mail. I dug underneath my skin to see if I was still there.

Through the door: No you can't take that away from me.

He moved toward me like a big-game hunter, and his

hunting skills were still shit. We could just fill the hole in, he said.

But my head, I said.

He held his hands out in front of him, a shield and distraction. Right now, he said. We can just fill the hole in. Easy.

All that work, I said.

I bet it was, he said, gentle, too gently.

I'm not crazy.

I know. But we can fill the hole in, put all this behind us.

And then what?

He leaned back, puffed out his cheeks, looked up at the sky. The sun will come up, he said. We'll take the day off. Stay in bed. Talk, read. Whatever you want. Sleep.

I can't sleep.

OK, he said. His new questions, new thoughts, moving across his face. His easy sleep, his easy contentment, his alone. OK, he said. Then we'll watch movies, order in pizza.

And then what?

We'll take the next day too, he said. The wind moved shadows across his wet cheeks.

I pictured it, the two of us in our bed, hiding from the world. Creating a burrow of our blankets, a place we could remember, a place we could start again.

But at some point he'd fall asleep, mid-sentence. And I'd be awake long after.

No, I said, and stepped into the hole.

*

Animals that hibernate: wood frogs. Deer mice. Squirrels. Hamsters. Bats. Bears.

I can't sleep, but maybe that means I've been saving up. Maybe now that I've got my hole in the ground, now that I've said goodbye to things above, I can slip into a summer's nap.

The man says I need to come out, put some clothes on, come with him to a doctor. He frets and cries, begs me to stop slicing, stop tearing, to remember. He speaks, and all the words blend together into a hum, like the buzz of a good synth and industrial beat.

Animals that cocoon: moths and wasps. Animals that chrysalis: caterpillars.

Maybe I've been building my cocoon, my body turning hard like a chrysalis. And maybe I'll break out soon.

OH BONDAGE, UP YOURS

ON THE NIGHTS MRS. WALLACE IS A MAN, SHE HOLDS HER bourbon in her right hand. Bootlegged, that bourbon. We worry, before these nights of Mrs. Wallace's parties, that her connections on the North Side won't deliver the stuff so surely. But Mrs. Wallace gets what she wants, even in this prohibition year of nineteen hundred and twenty four.

When rousing her from her evening nap, necessary for stamina on the nights she is a man, we bring Mrs. Wallace her bourbon. She is nearly seventy years of age, and we ask her how she feels upon waking.

"Woke up in my own bed and not in heaven or hell," she says. "That feels quite nice."

We nod our assent and relief.

We help Mrs. Wallace dress in white tuxedo with tails that trail to her calves, a rectangular hat over slicked-back gray hair. This, we think, this man's uniform, this will be the future attire for women. Now that we women, even we working women, can lawfully vote.

"No need anymore for the bondage of our clothing," Mrs. Wallace says as we right her bow tie. "The skirts and trussing that impede our work."

We nod agreement, thrilling to scent the scandal in her sentiment.

The white of the tux is a striking contrast to the deep black of Mrs. Wallace's skin. This deep black delights us, having known moneyed people to be only white, often having known white people only. We help Mrs. Wallace apply a dark kohl pencil above her lip, sketching a thin smart mustache. We are taller than our employer, and must lean down over her.

"All you young folk, bigger and bigger," she says. "All these giants we're breeding. Maybe one day people grow tall enough to surpass all the shit we step in now."

On the nights Mrs. Wallace is a man, she steps lighter, stands taller. We watch her gaze into the long looking glass in her room, slip her hands in her pockets and breathe deep.

"Pockets, ladies. Places for money, notes, keys. Notice how a man can carry his entire person upon himself all the time. No wonder they have such confidence. Pockets will be our next push."

Mrs. Wallace, on the nights she is a man, has the kind of self-assurance that's built and nurtured and stoked, like a fire puffed by a bellows. It is infectious, and we feel ourselves glowing too, royal like her.

*

On the days she is a woman, Mrs. Wallace holds her tea in her left hand. Prim and watered-down, the tea.

Standing before the portrait at the mantelpiece, she is curled and gnarled as a tree root, and her lips move.

We breathe rougher, our chests tight.

*

But on the nights she is a man, her grand Bronzeville brownstone fills with life and color. Mrs. Wallace hosts her South Side salon every month, bringing in guests like we had never before seen in our tenements and towns across the seas.

"I welcome here the artists," Mrs. Wallace tells us, "the beautiful and ugly, the talented and merely persistent, the oddities and the unfit. All who live unbound."

Mrs. Wallace describes them to us before they arrive, that we might provide each a more personal greeting. She quizzes us, that we may, without fail, identify the players on sight. It seems they all pour in at once, a bustle of hats and furs, pocketbooks and cigarettes, spurring us into motion to collect their belongings, naming each figure as they come.

Charlie Whitaker, a slight and icy blonde known for his flights across the ballet stage. Hume Roberts, his oiled black hair long in front but shaved, on the sides, to show his egg-blue skull. Susie Sweetcheeks, burlesque dancer, scarved in feathers, with sequins dangling across brown skin. Theodora O'Malley, attired somewhere between man and woman, in pageboy cap and suspenders, and demonizing Trotsky, lionizing Lenin, at top volume. S.S. Shepard, the poet, holding her cigarette cheek-high, made for the cinema with her smooth black boyishly short hair, her sharp angles and deep shadows.

In this grand parlor two dozen men and women in all manner of dress and undress, smoke clouding above their heads and illicit liquor wetting their lips. Mrs. Wallace, hands on hips, stands framed in her bay window above Cottage Grove Avenue, assessing the bunch.

"My licentious lords, my literary ladies. My pauper princes and prostitute princesses. My artistic attendants and suffragette squires. My people."

To the crowd she is sovereign. They address her as King, Your Majesty. We wonder at these Americans dubbing a negress a king, and we understand it too.

The subjects call out at the same moment each night, call for a story, and each night Mrs. Wallace manufactures the surprise that satisfies them.

*

On the days Mrs. Wallace is a woman, she crafts these stories. We bring her tea and lemon, watching as she wears her pencils down to shavings, wears a path of wood creaks and groans, whispering to herself all the time. We visit her sitting room that smells of wood and sweat and something sweet that reminds us of grandmothers gone. We inform her of breakfast, lunch, dinner, and bring her food on silver trays when she ignores us. We remind her of the need for sleep, and guide her to her sleigh bed when it is long night outside her windows.

Some days, and with increasing frequency, Mrs. Wallace receives her doctor, who asks her how she feels.

"I find I am now bound by an old woman's body. Meanwhile, my mind resides elsewhere, unencumbered. It's quite confusing."

The doctor, a kind man with whiskers and white ear hair, smiles at Mrs. Wallace like he might a child, advises her to rest, to receive fewer visitors, to reap the reward of her seventy-some years. He takes his leave, and Mrs. Wallace disappears for a time. Often we'll find her in her tux, even if it is not a night for visitors. We help her dress for bed. She tells us the same thing each time, pinching her arm and ours, in the fleshy part under the elbow.

"Doctors care about the meat. Men care about the shape. Whites care about the color. It's the body for women, even when we're old. No thought or care to what animates it."

*

But on the nights Mrs. Wallace is a man, she is revered rightfully as royalty, begged to tell her tales, and we watch her ritual call and response.

"And what story would you have?"

Someone in the crowd always squeals for a fair princess.

"Far too many of those. And we all know what happens to those princesses once they find their Charmings. Buggered in the ass."

Laughs ripple through the crowd. Someone, usually one of the men, requests a wicked queen.

"You'll know more about queening than I."

No doubt she is right. Finally, someone asks for a tale of the future.

"You want to hear of justice. Titans of industry thrown down, the meatpackers rising up. Our Chicago the new Bolshevik paradise. All us outcasts placed where we should be. But I have no such stories."

Mrs. Wallace, even as a man, is a realist.

"I will tell a tale of true future. What awaits us all, if we are so lucky. Will you hear it?"

Her subjects shout aye, and we fill their glasses with more bourbon.

"But beware. My tales are of truth, which is not the same as happiness. Prepare yourselves for a story of horror. A story of a woman grown old."

Much laughter comes, each and every night Mrs. Wallace is a man.

The stories vary but cleave to a theme. Mrs. Wallace tells of an old woman who falls down the stairs, only to use her resulting leg cast to cart contraband. Or an old woman watching as her children quibble over her fortune, revealing herself as a witch only when they reveal themselves as demons.

Mrs. Wallace performs, and then others follow. Miss Shepard reads a handful of odes to physical love, and her listeners fan themselves and sigh. Mr. Roberts monologues from his plays of tortured souls leading double lives, to shouts of bravo. Miss O'Malley stumps for the workers party, to polite applause and yawns. Mr. Whitaker and Miss Sweetcheeks dance a duet, both wearing too many clothes to dance free but blotted enough not to care.

Mrs. Wallace surveys her subjects, sometimes with a smile, sometimes with a grimace that tries to be more. She ends the performances with the same requiem each time.

"Who sings songs of us, friends? And the bravery of living each day? No one but us."

*

On the days Mrs. Wallace is a woman, we cook, bring her food, clean her cabinets and cupboards, polish her silver, dust her décor. We — Irish and Polish and Czech and Italian — prattle among ourselves in our home languages, and to each other in English thickly accented and metered out all wrong.

We picture our futures. We think of homes of our own, with American husbands and American children. Our own kingdoms, where we may do as Mrs. Wallace does. Where we have solved the mystery of how to obtain what we wish.

*

On most nights, after most of her guests leave, Mrs.
Wallace slips upstairs to find Miss Shepard waiting.
We are instructed not to wake them in the morning.

We servants come from rules, by men and God. We
come from stern mothers and severe mistresses and
scornful masters. We find respite in Mrs. Wallace's
kindness. Yet she sins so fully, so clearly. It is on these
nights we struggle, pray harder on our knees, willing
the sin to leave this house.

But sometimes, Miss Shepard leaves with the rest,
and we are happy. Mrs. Wallace sits downstairs in her
tux, slumped with fatigue yet breathing hard with
excitement. She watches while we scurry about,
cleaning up the detritus of her court.

"Shall I tell you girls a story?"

We stop to listen, knowing this means we will sleep
less for finishing our work later. But we stop.

"I tell that crowd tales of old women. But I don't talk
of what makes us old."

We sink to our knees easily, willingly.

Mrs. Wallace talks of slaves then, two who ran away
to the North. We know a bit about this, small nuggets
of this country's history. We also know other tales,
from our own families and our own lives, pogroms and
feudal landowners and war, always war. Mrs. Wallace
talks of the child they have, who runs away from
bondage as her parents did. We think of our own
running, the creaking, nauseous ships that carried us,

the cold but female statue that greeted us, the rattling, shrieking train that shuttled us across the country and into this city. We think also of Mrs. Wallace, of this house, of the people she consorts with, and we construct our own stories for her running.

Mrs. Wallace talks of the man above the mantelpiece, and from our seats on the oak floor we look up to the wall-size photograph. Mr. Wallace is a big bear of a man. He wears what appears to be a white tux with tails. He smiles, ignoring the standard of solemnity. Mrs. Wallace tells stories of her husband, the man who married her knowing who she was, the man who loved other men, the man who gave her this house before he died.

We struggle again, thinking of the prayers we will whisper on our knees, fierce.

Mrs. Wallace pauses for some time.

"When we traveled, through the three decades of our marriage, Mr. Wallace and I heard stories everywhere. We learned that other languages tell stories in words that are divided. In Spain, *la montana* means *the mountain*. A feminine word, for something that is part of creation, and will be here long after us. But *the future* is *el futuro*. A masculine word. It would always make me cry, thinking about that."

It is on these nights, the nights Mrs. Wallace is a man, when she speaks to us without shame, that we are brave. We do more than simply nod and behave kindly, as the help must do. We are women, dreamers.

"Mrs. Wallace..."

We struggle with our tongues, the syllables so different in our home languages. We try to translate our heads and hearts. We try to believe that this woman will understand dreaming, even from the help. We try to ignore the voice of our rules and mothers, who speak only of shame. When words fail us, we simply look at our Mrs. Wallace and pray she is the magic that we see.

But she smiles and shakes her head, at us silly girls who don't listen to the story.

*

On the mornings Mrs. Wallace is a woman, we hold our breath before we open her chamber door. We think of what Mrs. Wallace says on the nights she is a man.

"Remember how the world sees the future."

So we hold our breath, hoping to find the woman breathes freely.

THIS HUMAN FORM WHERE I WAS BORN

Four. The size in inches of the raw
discoloration on the right hip.

ANNIE'S BODY HAS AN OWNER NO LONGER. AFTER LEAVING
Gertie, her body tells her to return, to go back.
Her body puts her on the wrong train after work, the
blue one that takes her to Wicker Park and Gertie,
instead of the red one that takes her to her tiny, empty
studio in Uptown. She dreams of puzzles missing
pieces, socks without their pairs, graves on the edge of
cemeteries.

There's a night when Annie's friends take her out,
the friends still around since the divorce. Engaged
Anya and married Chanda and partnered Michael and
open-married Marcus. At dinner, ceviche and
margaritas with salted rims, they speak from a script.
What really happened, they ask. I can't believe it, they
say, which is also a question. Both sound like accusa-
tions.

Annie says they fought a lot, she and Gertie. More
than they let on.

Her friends fidget. Anya bites a purple-manicured nail on her wedding-china-white hand. Chanda nibbles her straw through too-white teeth and plum lips. Michael taps his pointy-toed loafer on the floor and his skeleton fingers on the table. Marcus checks his phone for Scruff hits on his BBD profile. In that fidgeting they ask questions that are not given voice. Aren't you supposed to persevere? Past the fights, the boredom, the disappointment?

Annie says she's sad and would like to change the subject. Her friends' relief is a mass exhale of tangy lime breath.

They eat, they drink. They cab to Boystown, Buddy's for the guys, then The Closet for the girls. There is dancing to Rihanna and Madonna and Ariana, drinking of vodka sodas and tequila shots. Annie becomes one of many twisting torsos spiraling across the tightly packed dance floor. She and her friends turn into strobes of smoke, and she waves arms above her head, watching her limbs lengthen with the black and white elegance of a Marlene Dietrich film. Her sweat smells sweet amongst the humid cloud of humanity, tinged with Coco Mademoiselle and the margarita salt. She is light as she bounces on her toes, insubstantial, incorporeal. She could leave her body behind on this dance floor, float between the speakers and the rafters, through the TVs playing a loop of pin-up pictures, beautiful butches and femmes, into the crisp autumn air, up to the stars hidden beyond the orange glow of street lights.

Her friends want to leave. But if Annie stops moving, she's afraid she will die.

One of the shapes surrounding her resolves into a recognizable form, and Annie sees black skin and a soft brown crown of hair. A short white tank top, tight high-waist jeans. Annie's hand meets round hips. She is happy the woman is soft where Gertie was muscle and bone. She is sad this woman does not have Gertie's shape.

Dancing in the space between the strobe. Drinking. Talking. Annie forgets the words as they leave her mouth and arrive in her own ears. The woman kisses Annie's neck, her lips, then pulls her off the dance floor. Annie screams over the music, a line that's been in her head all morning from an old Pixies song.

The woman leads Annie into a back storeroom, or maybe a closet or kitchen. Annie can't tell in the dark. Then the woman pulls up Annie's shirt and bra, tongues her breast, while also slipping a finger into her cunt. Annie breathes deep, leans back, stretches towards the tongue and finger. It's a comfort to know her body is real, that it's seen and felt. Annie feels a vibration, something searing, and for a moment she thinks it's a new form of release. She will have a new kind of orgasm to herald her new life and new lovers. But the woman extricates herself, jumping back with a shriek. She pulls Annie into the bathroom, her jeans around her knees and breasts out. The woman pushes Annie onto the lip of the grimy sink. Annie doesn't understand until she feels the cold water on her hip and looks down. There's a bright pink spot. The woman says something about a pipe, radiator, burn. Annie watches the water, waiting to feel it, feel the cool or the burn. Nothing. When she looks up the woman is gone.

The next morning Annie remembers the burn when she scrapes her underwear down her leg. She wants to vomit, but instead she applies Vaseline, unsure what else to do. Only after, as the burn stings and aches and hisses through her hip, does she remember the woman's tongue and finger. That at least is something.

Three. The height in inches of the subdermal black ink on the back left shoulder.

Every day on her walk home from the train, Annie passes a tattoo parlor on Broadway. Sometimes the door is open to the street, and she sees red walls and thumbtacked prints of comics. The speakers scream Social Distortion and Fugazi.

Gertie didn't like tattoos.

On the day the hum in her hip begins to recede, and the hum in her head returns, the one imploring her to go back home, Annie turns in through the door. There's a man with an orange clawed hand stretching across his neck. He guides her to a table that might have come from a gynecologist's office. On a neighboring table a college girl lies stripped to bra and jeans, a silent man chiseling a sword along her ribcage. Next to her a skate punk stripped to boxer briefs is getting a Lannister House sigil engraved on his thigh. No shyness or qualms in the name of art. Annie takes off her shirt.

The man who will mark her skin prepares his surgeon's plate of sterilized needles and guns. He keeps another one on his other side, for ink, gauze, and cream. Tattooists are not hair stylists. They don't want to know the mind inside the skin they carve. This claw-necked man is silent, and Annie, tired of talk, is happy.

The college girl emits a thin rattling whistle between gritted teeth. The skater tugs at his snapback hat with weed symbol, takes it off, folds it, dons it again, grimacing. There will be pain. It's what Annie expects, and without it she'd be disappointed. But she hates the firstness of this moment, wants it to be over.

Social Distortion stops and the room resonates with moans and gasps. A metal hum. From behind a tartan curtain a troll appears, elvish markings across his arms, legs, and shaved head. He shuffles to the counter in his board shorts and flip flops and pushes buttons. Then horns, and Otis Redding. Try a little tenderness, he sings. Annie's shoulders sink. She reclines again. That's when the machine awakens behind her ear and the needle bites into her back.

Annie breathes, a gasp and catch and stiffening. Painful, yes. But more.

The gun vibrates and the needle stabs in quick succession and the artist wipes away inky blood and there is nothing else she needs and nothing else she wants and nothing else to think. She remembers this feeling is called joy.

Otis sings, an entire album of pain and pleasure,

while the gun and the needle and the artist do their work.

Finally they're done. The tattooist wipes once and then gives Annie a mirror. A small black dove flies on her left shoulder. Cut her open and there it was.

Two. The centimeters disparity between the length of the legs, measured from hip socket to bottom of fibula.

Annie runs. It is Thanksgiving morning and it is snowing and she runs for an hour. She runs a rectangle from empty Uptown to quiet Lincoln Square to vacant Roscoe Village to silent Lakeview and back. Her earbuds pump out White Stripes and Peaches. Her left hip twinges in mile two, then pulses in mile four, then screams in mile six. During her two-block cool down, the music downshifts to Cat Power and she limps along to her howl about a metal heart not worth a thing.

This is not the first hip pain from running. But it is the worst. So Annie gives in this time and visits a doctor. The doctor sends her to a physical therapist. This therapist watches Annie walk and run on a treadmill. The therapist wears Lululemon pants and a hoodie, and speaks to the top of Annie's head, saying words like *IT band, excessive mileage, improper gait, misalignment, corrective exercises.*

Annie has been walking wrong her entire life, the therapist says. Annie's legs are of unequal length. Annie's body has finally had enough and must be heard.

Left alone a moment as the therapist writes up a

treatment plan, Annie thinks of pairs. Her legs, her arms. Her hands, her butt cheeks, her ears, her eyes.

Under the therapist's supervision, Annie practices balance exercises on a Bosu ball, rolls her legs with a foam roller, performs deadlifts and squats in slow motion to correct the form. She finishes sweaty and sapped.

The therapist has Annie lie down on a long rectangular table reminiscent of the tattoo table. The therapist folds Annie's left leg and pushes it into her chest, the therapist's face hovering over her. The therapist has a mole on her white forehead just above her penciled-in eyebrow, gold triangle earrings that dangle near her cheeks, blonde hair that curls over her ears. She looks nothing like Gertie. But in this moment there are two people, a pair, and they are touching limbs and can feel each other's breath.

Annie's hip throbs when she leaves, and her underwear is damp.

In her empty studio, on her emaciated futon, Annie stretches out her legs. She studies the different patterns of moles and freckles. One knee has a patch of brown hair she missed when shaving. She tries to eye the difference, perceive the extra length of the right leg beside the left. But they look the same.

Annie does the work, attends the appointments, until her insurance allotment runs out. But the work doesn't take. She walks instead of runs. Her mismatched limbs no longer respond to her commands.

One. Toe with an empty nail bed.

Engaged Anya and partnered Michael and open-
married Marcus gather at married Chanda's condo in
Humboldt Park. It is mid-December and this is a
holiday party with a large invite list. Spouses and
significant others will be at this party. Annie drinks
three gin and tonics at home before her Lyft arrives.

Chanda and her husband are agnostic, but in their
den they have a real pine with string lights, stockings
above the stairwell, Bing Crosby on the Bluetooth
speakers. Sequin dresses and tights on the women,
sweater vests and oxfords on the men. Annie wears
Converse and a knitted hat topped with a pom.

There is apple cider and bourbon, and on her third
mug Annie talks to Chanda's brother Chase. He is
asking about Gertie, and Annie shakes her head and
drinks the shot she poured along with her cocktail. No
really, Chase says, his twenty-something white male
face a blank space on which she can paint her own
pattern. Tell me, he says.

And she does. Annie tells Chase that she'd been in
love, or at least convinced herself she was, and really,
what was the difference? What you *think* you feel, you
feel, she says. But that feeling, that belief in a feeling,
changed. There wasn't a specific event to point to, she
says. She and Gertie argued about what mattress to
buy, what shade of gray to paint the condo's living
room, the right amount to spend on a bottle of whiskey.
Occasionally they yelled at one another, when they

couldn't yell at their supervisors and parents and elected leaders, and most of the time they understood this need to vent, this role that they played for each other, and any resentment and hurt feelings could be forgiven. But they stopped surprising each other. Consistency is comfort, Annie says. It's nice to know what to expect. But, for example, the punctuality of their weekly sex — Wednesday at 10:00 p.m. following an early dinner and movie in Streeterville — became a series of known steps, all enacted in the same order for the same amount of time. Like laundry or an annual Pap smear.

Really, Annie says to Chase, the things she liked changed. Ten years is enough time for that to happen. Dairy and steampunk and mid-century design, all things she loved at 25. Things she couldn't stomach at 35. Gertie was one of those things.

That's depressing, Chase says. Annie says yes. Aren't you supposed to change together? Annie says yes.

They drink to the disappointment of reality. They keep drinking, as the music gets louder and segues to disco, as the veneer of mid 30s adulthood slips from the people in the room and they remember what it feels like to party without responsibility. Vests are shed along with shoes and there are shots and dance-offs. Someone, breaking the rule about smoking only on the step-out Juliet balcony, lights up in the living room.

Chase and Annie are wedged together into a corner. He's speaking into her ear and his lips brush her hair and cheek. It's been a long time since Annie flirted with a man, had sex with a man — college perhaps. She always appreciated the beauty of some men, even their cocks, brainless worms that they were. She could appreciate them even if she preferred the shapes of women. She puts a hand on the front of Chase's pants, feels his outline through the poly cotton blend.

After a moment in which they gape at one another like witnesses to a three-second knockout while Annie holds her breath and Chase gasps, he pulls them into the hall. He grabs her hand and sticks it down his boxers. Her senses are heightened yet slowed, so it takes a moment for her to grip, to feel it grow. A kind of victory, the speed at which his body responds to hers.

And it's fine, and she thinks it might be fun to feel the tip of his penis nudging around her vagina in the way that they do. But Annie also feels nauseous, the bourbon returning. She pulls her hand away, her nails scraping him, and he yelps. She run-stumbles, her left Converse coming loose, to Chanda's personal vanity and shower. Her left foot wedges under the thin particle board door of the bathroom. Something rips, and there's stabbing pain in her toes, but she's got a bigger problem, and it's coming up her throat in a hot gush. Her vomit just misses the toilet, spraying the tile and shower curtain.

Ah fuck, Chase says. He's followed her, the perfect gentleman, and she looks up to see him dry heave and turn his back.

Annie winds wads of toilet paper around her hand and pools the puke. She stops to vomit again, in the commode this time. Chase says he has to go, apologizes. Annie thinks the apology might be to himself, to his body, his squeamishness getting in the way of sex.

She splashes water on her face and rinses her mouth. Notices red on her foot. Peels back her argyle sock and brings her big toenail with it, stuck in the fabric like a macabre brooch. Her toe is all red and now she feels the full hot pulse of it. She cries as she curls her leg over the sink, runs cool water over her foot. She finds hydrogen peroxide in the medicine cabinet and bites down on her palm when it sears her toe. She picks the nail off her sock, and puts the scaly thing back on her toe. Binds it together with gauze and tape from the cabinet.

This is not an adult solution. Her toenail will not reattach and grow like a lizard regrowing a tail. But Annie is surrounded by adults who are pretending they are young again, who have forgotten their world weariness and ready answers for crises. And she is not an adult.

Annie decides she will handle this tomorrow. A solution will come to her then. She leaves the party without speaking to Chase Chanda Anya Michael Marcus all busy losing their minds.

At home, Chase texts her. Asks if she's feeling better. If she wants to meet some other time. Annie blocks him from her phone, changes her bandage and hopes for sleep to heal.

Zero.

On the train home. The right one, the red one. A few days before Christmas. Annie is staying in the city this year, the idea of the pity at home too much. Her parents and their spouses had been slow to warm to Gertie, girl that she was, phase that they thought she was. But now. To be alone at 36. Disaster.

Annie is thinking of Gertie, listening to Henry Rollins scream in her ear buds about being a liar. She is thinking of the shit year it's been. She is thinking in her loop when the ache in her chest, the one that's been there all day, gets bigger. Louder. It covers the area under her breasts, into her armpits, under her lateral wings.

And then her knees give out. She kneels on the floor, the curved metal cutting into the flesh of her calves. She's unable to catch her breath, but at the same time she's inhaling the stench of piss and bile and slush down there, the stuff that no amount of industrial cleaner can erase from these train floors. Sweat pops under her bra line and down her back, pouring from her hairline. Someone says words to her, but she can't see this someone, can only see the vague outline of their shape against the growing black of her vision.

The train pulls into Belmont, and Annie finds adrenaline and fear ready, pushing her off the floor and onto the newly expanded platform. She sprints down the newly metal stairs. Something is going to explode and she's not sure what or what direction it will be, but

Masonic is two blocks away. She runs the long, long city blocks to Wellington, and for a moment feels happy that she is running again, freedom and power, and she runs east and spots the ER and activates the sliding doors and stops inside and pants and her bladder lets go a little before reasserting control and she sweats and sweats and the hall is turning black and she feels hollow and Annie feels another body keeping her steady, strong arms that gently guide her on quivering legs to a plastic chair. Someone gives her water, and points a tiny desk fan at her face. Over long seconds, Annie's sweat cools, and her breath slows. Someone, maybe the same someone with gifts, asks what happened, how she's feeling. Words come out of Annie's mouth and she thinks they are the right ones.

There are tests, cuff on her arm, syringe in her elbow, electrodes on her chest. All of them come back to smiles from nurses and technicians and doctors.

Anxiety, they say. Panic. That's all. The body does funny things, they say. When it's under pressure. But zero heart irregularities.

Annie is not relieved, as perhaps she should be. This should have been a heart attack. That thing in her chest should be shocked and broken. It should be reshaping itself. It should look different and act different and be different. Her heart's resilience isn't fair, the regularity isn't right.

The doctor hands her a prescription for Lorazepam. Ten pills, without a refill. Annie wonders if it's enough, if ten will do the trick of shutting this body down for good. She may have said some of this out loud, for the doctor narrows his eyes, takes the slip of paper back. Tells her to hang on a sec.

When he's gone, Annie slips out the sliding door.

In her studio she lies on her futon. For a long while, she doesn't move, simply breathing and taking small pleasure in the lack of pain. Her eyes are open, and she charts the stipple on the ceiling, the small bubbles and patterns that form a sort of constellation.

Late in the evening, she gets up and eases onto her feet. In a slow, careful trip to the bathroom, she assembles her tools. The cream she eventually found to soothe her burn. The lotion to keep her tattoo supple and bright. The tennis ball she rolls over her hip joints to ease the strain. The new bandage for her toe bed.

Annie fingers her brands and scars. She hums as she works, the line from the Pixies song, but also bits of other songs, and sounds that come to her from nowhere. She hums and hums, making it up as she goes, waiting to see what's next.

DOUBLE DARE YA

WE THREE SAT AT OUR WINDOW TABLE AFTER LUNCH OF turkey pot pie, drinking lemon ginger tea for digestion.

"We call it moonrise," Maude said. She spoke low, and I leaned forward. Elbows on the paisley tablecloth, socked feet hovering over the checked carpet, backside aching from the poorly cushioned wooden chairs.

"Why moonrise?" I pulled my cup to my mouth, then pushed it away just as quickly. My favorite tea, but today the smell made my stomach churn.

"Because of menses," Abigail said. "We never called our monthlies that, of course. But the word, *menses.* It comes from *moon.*" She wiped at the corners of her mouth, the only place on her face where the wrinkles settled deep, then patted the gray fuzz circling her head.

We quieted as the men at the table next to us began the slow process of rising to their feet, steadying, and shuffling toward the exit. Everything pained, slow bodies working around worn joints and thinned bones.

I tried the tea again, pushed it away again.

"Happened to me too, Leslie," Maude said. She

pointed to my tea, then her nose. "My smell went funny around the time the changes started. It passes." Her face was all wrinkle and sag, white skin folded over itself and mottled with moles, but her nose was long and smooth.

"What's happening to us?" For weeks I'd been wanting to ask them this. We'd known each other a year now, since Donald's health started to fail, since he and I sold the house and moved into the Lazy Acres Assisted Living Community. I'd wanted to ask, but feared laughter or pity. More, I feared that this thing, this strange new something, was the sign of decline, finally coming for me.

Now Abigail placed a gnarled brown finger, big-knuckled and bony, on the laminate table. "We get our monthlies when we're little. I was thirteen." She moved her finger across, a gap of inches. "Then they leave us when we're in our fifties. And then what? Past was, we'd die long before that." Her finger moved again, another gap. "But here we are. In our eighties. Goddamn 2015. Our men gone. And…" The finger lifted, and her hand flipped, holding something invisible.

"What?" I watched her hand, and for a second could swear I saw something circular, clear, a cylinder of sorts. Then it disappeared, and only Abigail's light brown palm remained.

"We've always been the strong ones, haven't we?" Maude leaned forward again, and Abigail and I did likewise. I saw us from above: we were like girls at the cafeteria lunch table, huddled over secrets and scandals. Teenagers talking about the new blood they'd shed. Middle-aged mothers, gabbing at church potlucks, commiserating over the hot flashes that drove us to the freezer. Now shrunken widows. And we finally had something truly secret to whisper about.

"Of course," Abigail said, adjusting the thick frames that magnified her black eyes. "We've always been stronger than our men. Doing what needs done. Eugene could lift any furniture I'd set him to, but face our Lanie's chemo treatments? See our daughter lose chunks of hair and wither away? Hell no."

Maude nodded, her pale chin loose and wobbly. "Ask Perry to fix our lawnmower, sure. Ask him to watch me have his children, and he faints."

I thought about Donald, his calves and forearms. They had been so round, so meaty. Seeing him at our church, near the end of my senior year of high school, I'd pointed him out to my girlfriend. That's a man, I said. I thought we would be a unit, Donald and Leslie, under his protection. I hadn't yet seen how muscles could be like makeup, the things we girls used to hide our flaws.

"So we've always been strong," I said. "True. But…"

"Not like this," Maude said, smoothing her zip-up hoodie down her sides.

The tea had grown cold. The cup was almost industrial in its plainness, the beige the color of boredom, the sturdy plasticized edges resistant to shatter. I pictured these cups as two-for-one at some

79

old-folks-home supply store, along with plastic runners for the hallways and grip bars in the showers.

"For some of us," said Abigail, those giant insect eyes bearing down on me. "There's a third phase nobody talks about."

The tea. That damn cup. Anonymous, ordinary. Picked for people on their way out. Just looking at it made my stomach twitch and turn. I raised a hand above my head and waved, like I was a queen, dismissing someone who disappointed her.

Then the cup was gone, the dirt-colored water gone, the smell gone. Vanished.

I looked for it, on the floor, on another table. When I couldn't find it, I looked at my friends.

Maude and Abigail didn't move, but their lips curled back into toothy grins.

*

He had died in his sleep a month ago. It's what we all hope for. And that morning as I sat beside Donald's cooling body, my mind still gummy from sleep, I resented him that. Why a peaceful, merciful end for him?

I poked at his cheek, his neck, his skinny arms. Pushed harder. Pinched and twisted.

His calves and forearms had long since wasted away, hanging from his legs like stretched-out rubber bands. His strong black curls had grown gray and lank. His mind was pricked with pinholes that grew larger every day. When I'd bring him meals from the cafeteria, I might find him hard and sharp, seated in his chair and nodding along to a sermon or Fox News blast on TV. Or I might find him with kind eyes and a smile. Then I'd linger and turn the TV off. I'd hold his hand, wipe his chin, kiss his soft forehead, slightly salty. It was irresistible to see: this must have been what he was like as a baby, before he assumed the mantle of manhood.

But still, he had finally passed peacefully.

That first week, I made myself wear black, through the wake and funeral. At the graveside, I held my daughter Heidi's hand, and she held her daughter Nora's hand. At the reception, people praised our strength. No tears to be seen.

The second week, I made myself go through his things, holding each shirt for a long minute, sniffing out sorrow like a cat her litter. I packed up all the shirts, slacks, and shoes, the toys, devices, and gadgets, the rules, rules, rules. Manny, the Guatemalan handyman whom Donald would scream at whenever a light bulb needed changing or toilet handle fixing, took away the boxes. He gave my hand a gentle squeeze, and wished me all of God's blessings during this hard time. I bit my cheeks and nodded.

When he was gone, and all of Donald with him, I shut and locked the door to our unit. Now my unit. In our bedroom, now my bedroom, I grabbed a pillow, stuffed it against my mouth. After a few seconds I heard meaty, wild sounds that tore tears from my eyes, stole breath from every corner of my body. Laughter. Laughs that, for a second, I thought might kill me. And how would that be as a way to go?

My hands gripped the pillow, squeezing, kneading. And then they were tearing, the cloth ripping in half like tissue paper. The stuffing exploded, the clumps of poly cotton blend dancing on the air like dandelion fluff.

No one would complain about the mess. Not anymore. No one would complain about any mess, or the dry steak at dinner, or the poor calls of the college football coach, or the decayed morals of the people who wore jeans at church, or the lies of the *Des Moines Register* promoting the gay agenda. No one would complain about my behavior, or make demands, or mete out punishment.

Three things happened very quickly. I cramped, my gut seizing so that my body curled around it. Then I flushed, sweat popping from my pores and soaking my shirt. Then I came, my back arching, legs stretching, head rolling.

I must have fainted for a second because I opened my eyes to see the ceiling. There was a fleck of paint directly above me, a spot of blue on the white. I blinked, and it was closer. I blinked again, and saw the spot's rounded edges formed a pentagon. Blinked, and I saw what the ceiling hid, pipes and wiring and insulation. One more blink, and I saw only blue sky.

I shook my head. Maybe Donald's decay had been contagious.

Getting to my feet was easy, and that task hadn't been easy for a long time. My legs felt strong and sure as they carried me to the living room.

Donald's recliner sat there like a throne. Such an ugly thing, cheap cracked leather and sweat-worn arms. I'd read that mattresses get heavier over time, collecting dead skin cells. We molt, like snakes and birds. That recliner carried pounds of Donald.

I picked it up. My body carried eighty-two years and ninety pounds and five feet. I'd long since stopped picking up things that didn't fit in the palms of my hands. But I picked the recliner up like it was a beige plastic cup, carried it to our spare room, put it down, and covered it with a quilt.

I stared at that chair a long time, then at my hands. They looked the same, spotted and knobby. But they felt fuller somehow. Tingling, like they were coming awake from a long time asleep.

*

After I made my tea disappear, we went and sat on Maude's concrete rectangle outside her unit, a four-by-six allotment that comfortably accommodated two chairs, three in a squeeze.

Maude held a cigarette between her second and third fingers, the ash growing. My fingers itched, wanting one. But I'd had to give it up years ago. We all did.

I told Maude and Abigail about the strange fits of strength, and how, after that first time, I woke the next morning sore and weak. But within days I'd rearranged the living room and relocated the bed without grunt or pain.

"That's just the start." Abigail held her hand aloft again. There was another shadow above her palm, a shape that teased me before disappearing. "Have you seen things?"

I nodded.

"Have you seen people?" Maude spoke quietly around her puff of ashy air.

"What do you mean?"

"I always had a bit of sight, when I was younger," Abigail said. "Like the time I had a strong notion that something was wrong. For weeks, I couldn't shake it. Then Lanie was in the hospital. They'd just found her cancer."

I remembered then. Feelings, instincts, over the years. Knowing Heidi had something big to tell us before she called to announce her pregnancy. Knowing the police would find something vile in the neighbor's house before they discovered the cache of children's photos. Knowing the outlines of things.

"It wasn't useful, though," said Maude. "I knew in my gut that Perry was sleeping with other women, but couldn't do nothing about it. I was just imagining things, according to him. Acting crazy."

"Right," Abigail said, lighting up her own cigarette and sinking into her chair. "We'd just be overreacting, trying to get attention."

"But now it's different," Maude said.

"Detailed," Abigail said. "Specific. And we can control it."

"You know what we mean?"

I let loose the breath I'd been holding.

I remembered the volunteer, a gap-toothed teenage boy, from a week past. He'd caught my eye while clearing our cafeteria table. I saw him, and something inside told me to keep looking. So I did. And then came a vision of him in one of the other rooms: an engagement ring and gold chain in his hand, he'd stuffed them into his pocket. Just then the front desk staffer came into the cafeteria, on the hunt, and pulled the boy aside. Everybody heard later he'd stolen jewelry from a couple near their end.

On Maude's porch, Abigail nodded. "We've always seen more than people think," she said. "Our whole lives."

"Now we see even more," Maude said.

I looked past them, towards the golf course next door. A handful of raisined men in knee socks stood circled on the course's edge. They craned their necks, hands on canes or walkers.

"Look at that smile, Abigail," Maude said. "This one sees plenty."

*

The next day, we went to Walmart on the weekly Lazy Acres bus trip. Dozens of elderly women and a few men set loose for an hour to pick up the necessities.

There's a humor to it, Maude and Abigail said. Like there *is* someone up there, something conscious, with a sense of irony. Letting us have fun.

"See what their eyes do?" Maude pointed to a group of men, perhaps in their twenties, backwards caps and board shorts, picking over the cases of beer. Maude waved to them and, drawn to movement, the pack looked our way. But their gazes only glanced, hopscotching over us to the TV display, the stack of "As Seen on TV" items, then back to their beer.

"We've been invisible for a long time now," Abigail said, performing her own wave. The men didn't look this time.

"It's the young who are seen," Maude said.

I watched the boys-pretending-to-be-men as they spotted a woman in tight, shaped yoga pants. They puffed up, the boys, growing taller with their leering. When she heard their whistle, saw their attention, she shrank, curling into herself.

"I remember when I knew I was officially old," Maude said. She pointed to her chest, two ample breasts held in place by what I imagined was a heavily wired bra. "These things always got notice. Until I was about forty or so. You know how you can tell someone is looking at you? That sort of itchy feeling? It went away."

"Black like me, I always had that feeling," Abigail said. "Walk in a store, walk down the street, all eyes. Waiting for something wrong to happen. Until I was about fifty. Then I became just some harmless piece of scenery."

I saw my own moments. The McDonald's employee who called me ma'am for the first time. The grizzled man in camouflage who barreled into me at Quik Trip, apologized with confusion. The clerk at Menard's, who looked at me and a teenage Heidi with a gaze driven by genetics, a biological need to identify the best of the species, and settled on Heidi with an abrupt finality.

In the Walmart aisle, Maude and Abigail both, as one, placed fingers to their lips. They breathed in tandem, a gigantic intake of mutual air. And then they were gone.

I spun in place, like a cartoon. I walked up and down the aisle, peered over a shelf.

I waited, listening.

Then I reached out my hand, and felt solid bone and tissue.

Abigail laughed, and they were there again.

"See what we mean?"

They showed me how. Just a bit of thought, a bit of focus, and I could make myself truly unseen. I winked in and out of view, disappearing from the toilet paper display in the Walmart to reappear by the row of toothpastes, vanishing from the lunch meats to arrive again by the boxed wines. We chased each other through the backs of the aisles, following the laughter, breathless as children.

*

A bit of thought, of focus, and we could lift things, bend things, manipulate things.

I could make my phone move into my lap without a touch.

I could see people in their heads, see what they hid.

I could break my china, and fix it, all at once.

At night, I lay in my bed and thought about all the things I could do now. Options, choices, buzzing in my brain. That unfamiliar tingle.

But after weeks of playing with the power, I began to feel restless.

"What's the point?"

Maude and Abigail were in my living room, drinking gin in tumblers of ice and smoking marijuana. Maude got medical-grade for her arthritis, even though she'd already knitted her joints and ligaments back into working order. We'd held hands and worked our interiors early on, clearing our lungs of smoky clouds from past two-pack-a-day habits, straightening our curved spines, re-lubricating dried collagen and synovial fluids, filling up our hollow bird bones. We'd neutralized viruses waiting to be discovered, cut out cancerous moles, repopulated guts with good bacteria and unclogged our veins from cholesterol.

"This is the point," Abigail said, holding her breath, then expelling smoke and a laugh.

"But," I said.

"Leslie, we get to do what we want now," Maude said. She offered me the joint and I shook my head. She shook her own. "You're still thinking about rules.

About things we should and shouldn't do. We don't have to anymore."

"When's the last time, before all this, that you did something just because you wanted to?" Abigail stretched her arms high over her head and smiled. "I couldn't do this a year ago. My body wouldn't listen to me. Now it does. Because I tell it to."

"Shouldn't we, I don't know, use this somehow?"

"We are using it," Maude said. "We're healing ourselves."

"What do we tell our family?" I thought of Heidi and Nora, who might eventually notice my rising health.

"This is ours, no one else's," said Abigail, gritting her teeth.

I looked out through my patio door. Around the courtyard sat all our peers, husks made of papery skin and gummy bones, some connected to IVs and respirators, some asleep, or dead. All of their bodies filled with broken things, things that might be fixed.

"Why us?" I asked the glass. I knew we were the only ones in Lazy Acres. We could sense one another, anywhere at any time. We didn't sense anyone else. And even out in the world, at Walmart, at the gas station, at restaurants Heidi took me to when she visited, I didn't feel anyone like me.

"There's no shame in doing what you want, Leslie." Abigail stood next to me in the door frame. I wondered how she knew my shame. She was the harder one of the two. Burying a daughter and husband in the same year would do that. She told me once she'd always felt like a turtle, the soft head that led the way but hid under too much scrutiny. When her family died, she became the shell.

But now she patted my hand, then let hers stay there for a bit.

"Think of it this way," she said. "We used to be tied to the moon, for decades. I know, science may not agree there, but some things are beyond science. So every month our wombs were puffing and bleeding. Then we lost our connection to it, and there was nothing to do but shrink and shrivel. Watch ourselves die."

I looked up. The sun was bright, but I still could spot the outline of the moon in the eastern sky.

"The moon is locked by tides," I said.

"What's that now?"

"We always see the same side of the moon. The gravity of the earth and its tides keeps it there."

"Well now," Abigail said, smiling. "You know more about this than you think."

"My daughter does," I said.

I'd taken Heidi to an observatory once, I told them. Donald stayed home, insisting that looking for heaven through a telescope was dangerously close to pride. He was just transitioning then, from his long nights in bars to nights with his prayer group. But she was in junior high, and they were doing a class project on constellations.

Usually quiet, Heidi was a chatterbox that night, pointing to all the stars and naming them, reciting distances between bodies, describing light speed. We'd looked closely at the moon, near full. The gravity of the tides locked it, Heidi told me

"You know," I'd said. "When the moon is full, strange things happen. Emergency rooms fill up. People have seizures. More babies get born."

"That's not true," she said. And she had a kind of authority, through the crooked baby teeth and brown braids, the skinny legs with scabs on the knee.

"Sure it is," I said. "And women. We can feel the moon more than men."

"How?"

It was nearly time for the birds and bees, the talk of blood, of becoming a woman — but not yet. "You'll see."

"Mom. You can't just talk without proof."

"Don't you think your mom knows things?"

It impressed me even then, seeing her cutting look, the one that said she knew more than I did, the one that said she'd be more than me.

And she did and would, pushing past Donald's objections. It was 1974, she told him as she applied to colleges. Women could do things now, she said, as if that fact would turn a switch in his brain, inspire change rather than fear. As if that fact would change my life too. She went to college on a full academic scholarship, then to graduate school, where she was one of a few women to earn a doctorate in physics. She got research grants, awards, professorships. All of which Donald ignored each time we saw her, asking instead about potential husbands.

I'd tell her to ignore her father, who just had a hard time showing his love.

"It's not love when you don't even know someone," Heidi said. She was thirty then, just a few years from taking over the physics department at Michigan, and a few more from getting pregnant from an unknown source, announcing that she would raise the child on her own. Donald would refuse to see her, or our grandchild, a beautiful and smart girl named Nora, so I would meet them in secret. Until his dementia made rules null and void.

"Of course he knows you," I said. But later I would think back on that statement and hate myself for the lie.

"He has an image of a good daughter, and I'm not it," Heidi said.

I said something vague, conciliatory.

"The world is much bigger than him, Mom." She pointed up, in the direction of the moon and stars. "Bigger than what we know of life. We may see the same side of the moon through a telescope every time we look. But what's on the other side? What don't we see?"

I looked then, and saw only darkness.

On the patio, with Abigail, we were silent for a moment.

"We're connected again." She pointed up, somewhere above us, and then to the ground, the green of July. "To what's up there and what's down here. We have the power to do what we want."

"But we only feel it if we're free." Maude said from

behind us, pulled a deep drag into her lungs, and I watched the ash grow. "Well and truly free. No more husbands to take care of. Or kids. No more responsibilities. People making our meals and taking care of our bodies. No more women's work."

"All that old life gone," Abigail said.

"But then what?" I said.

"Leslie, what do you want?" Maude said.

They watched me struggle, comb through my mind and heart and come up empty.

*

The girls drank their gin as the afternoon waned, and smoked another joint. We held hands, repaired the damage to our livers, cleaned the room, then said goodnight.

Lying in bed I thought about power. I thought far back to history classes, the ones I didn't sleep through. I thought back through decades of news reports. Remembered lectures by Heidi when she deemed my understanding of an issue unsatisfactory. Kings used to call their power over their subjects absolute, ordained by God, allowing for any and every action for and against those subjects. Warriors used swords and guns and drones as power over other people. Men created laws to make their power dominant, keeping down others who were unlike them. So much effort and blood to claim power.

93

But all that was just machinery and messaging. Their power wasn't innate.

The next day, Maude's daughter Melanie came to visit. She drove our trio to lunch at Olive Garden. She and her husband would soon be leaving for a cruise to Cozumel for their 20th anniversary, she said, flipping her two-toned hair, rattling her charm bracelets, twisting the rings on each finger. I looked deeper, and saw that she'd caught him with the boy next door, a college sophomore home for break. Maude saw too. But we nodded, smiled, wished them the best time.

After, we stopped at Barnes and Noble. Abigail read cozy mysteries, tore through the cat-covered whodunits with elderly detectives at two a week, and Maude read the bodice-rippers, pirates and wenches on the covers. I wandered, eventually finding my way to the comic book section.

I flipped through a few. Heidi had never had much interest as a child, always so serious, idolizing inventors and pioneers. But I knew the gist. Powers came from radioactive spiders in these books, from science experiments gone wrong. They flew, they fought, they smashed. All in the name of truth, justice and the American way. They hid their true identities, but welcomed fame for their costumed alter egos.

Their power was all theatre. Manmade. Unnatural.

On the way back to the entrance, I walked by a display for teens. "If you liked Harry Potter," the sign read. The books were covered with boys and girls wielding wands and curling over cauldrons. I remembered a movie I'd watched with Heidi, women burned alive, branded as witches, for seduction, for spells, for communing with animals and dancing naked in the woods.

Their power, whether real or imagined, still had to play by rules.

I begged off from the girls that night, lay in my bed, sideways across the mattress as I'd taken to doing. I thought about all the things I could do now. Options, choices, buzzing in my brain. An unfamiliar tingle.

*

When Heidi came to see me that weekend, I offered her a drink.

"Are you serious?"

"What?" I held my half-finished gin and tonic in one hand, an empty glass in the other.

She smiled. "I've just never seen you drink much, Mom. Let alone offer it."

I shrugged. I poured her one and topped off my own, then joined her on the couch.

Her eyes were on me, itching.

"What is it?"

"You just look good, Mom." She put her drink on her knee. She was almost sixty now, but looked bright and lean, like years weighed little on her. Like she har-nessed the universe she taught and researched, and its light lived in her.

"And you, kiddo. Always."

"I wondered, you know. How you would do after Dad went. I knew he would go first. I was never quite sure what would happen to you then."

"And?"

. She raised her eyebrows, the smile still there. "I don't want to be disrespectful. But you look healthier and happier than I think I've ever seen."

"Since when do you care about being respectful?"

She laughed, and I joined her. "I just meant, I wanted this to be how you reacted. I wanted you to feel..."

"Free?" It was a surprise, hearing myself say it. It surprised her, too.

"Yeah," she said.

We sat for a moment, sipping our drinks.

"He was a bully," she finally said.

"He was."

"I tried to be sadder when he died. I really did."

"I know." I stopped there. Thinking the thoughts was enough.

"I've always wanted to ask why," Heidi said, speaking to her glass. "Why you stayed. Especially..."

I knew what she was thinking, because I could see it — in her mind, but also in mine, played in dual stereo. The night of the observatory, when we came home. He'd lapsed, skipping prayer for the bar. He yelled. I told her to go to her room, but saw her on the stairs, watching, before his fist closed my eyes.

There were other nights, too.

"I don't have a good answer. Not the one you or I want, anyway."

She wiped her thumb across the glass.

"I thought it would be done, when I got out of that home," she said. She looked quickly at my eyes, then back down. "But there's guys like him everywhere. Maybe not the same tactics. But even scientists."

I rifled through her head. Saw the things she hadn't told me, the panels made of men, labs filled with them, the talking to her breasts, the gossip she'd walked in on, the reduced salary, tiny cuts that she scabbed over.

"What kills me, though, is the younger generation. I thought for sure she wouldn't have to deal with the things we did."

"Nora?"

She exhaled hard, and her empty fist tightened. She nodded, and I saw: after Donald's funeral, the two of them at their home. Nora cried. Heidi, free of tears or guilt, asked why, since Nora's grandfather never asked or tried to be part of her life. Nora told her.

I felt very still, very cold.

Nora's boss, at the advertising agency where she interned. There were texts. Implications. Times when he touched her shoulders without needing to, lingering. Things Nora batted aside respectfully, carefully. But that only increased the volume, the thrill of the chase, the cornering of prey. He drew her a future, a career, with him. Drew its inverse, without him.

Heidi and I sat in silence on the couch. Her straw squeaked as she reached the end of her drink.

Nora would be OK, I told Heidi. She looked at me a moment, seeing something on my face. Then her smile, warm, dismissive. The adolescent, the college-bound prodigy, knowing her mother's power was nonexistent. But she thanked me, and we talked about nothing, the balance restored.

*

I thought about choices, in my bed, alone, awake, the courtyard lights drowning out the moon.

I thought about that song, the one Abigail kept playing on her boombox, the one that had wormed its way into my head, daring me.

I thought about what I wanted.

That's how I presented it to them. And their assent was instant. Curled eyebrows. Wide grins that matched mine.

"Look at that smile, Maude," Abigail said. "This one finally gets it."

*

We planned. We researched. We practiced. We waited, watching the sky.

We walked out of Lazy Acres on the night of the new moon, hidden by night's darkness and our own will, invisible to all but ourselves.

We walked miles on strong legs.

We walked fast, so fast our feet left the ground.

We found his house, a brick two-story in a

neighborhood of homes known for their mid-century style.

We entered his house. He slept upstairs, and he did not wake.

We walked the rooms. He'd furnished the house with knockoffs, copies of things popular when we three were young, starting our married lives, crafting a home, creating children, disappearing.

We picked locks, pulled out drawers, pocketed photos. He had copies of ID badges from his company, all girls, all Nora's age or slightly older. They looked like the staged, awkward settings of school photos, the same mix of embarrassment and pride.

We examined what we found. We looked into each other's heads. We were convinced, and resolved.

We climbed the stairs, our feet hovering over the old wood that might have announced our presence.

We moved, one by one, into his bedroom, and stood at the foot of his bed. We saw him clearly in the dark, the sheets thrown off in the throes of a dream. The bald head, with red hints of alopecia; the small, feminine nose; the sharp incisors; the wiry gray hairs on his bare, sunken chest; the thin, drooping thing between his chicken legs.

We waited, letting our presence fill the air, penetrate his nostrils, his pores.

We watched as he finally blinked, twice, before gasping, scrabbling, curling back against his headboard.

We saw ourselves as he saw us. Huge, towering statues, crones and queens. We let him fear us, let that fear fill his veins and take his breath. We grew taller in that fear, felt ourselves get stronger. We felt our power fill the final spaces of our bodies.

We threw the pictures at his feet.

We watched his eyes roll back. He sputtered out words, sounds meant to explain his actions and his impulses, meant to protect him.

We did not move.

We watched him gain his footing again, as he remembered this was his house, that he was a man, he was a boss, he made women obey. He spit out more words, sounds designed to cut at us, make us small, reassert the balance of power.

We smiled.

We dug into the soft, pulsing matter in his skull.

Stop, he said.

We watched in his head, watched the girls come and go, his slow sizing up of each challenge, his advertiser's skill of finding the soft spot, the insecurity, the flaw, the subtle mirror he held to it. And the sell: himself, their savior, their solution. Sometimes they accepted his sell. Sometimes they fought.

Stop, he said.

We held up our hands, and in each there was the shadow of something circular, clear, cylindrical. Something celestial. We poured ourselves into that shape, focused all our will and fury into it.

Stop, please, he said.

We forced his hands down from his eyes. He would see what we would give him.

Please, he said, a long pleading syllable.

We burrowed into his head.

We picked. Pinched. Penetrated his brain.

We poured the contents of our hands into a vein in his skull, watched as it formed a bubble of air pressing against the wall, bulging, threatening to burst.

Please, he screamed.

We looked at our fingers, puckered and chapped, bathed in detergent and bleach, the dried sheep hair in knitting needles. They felt full, our fingers. Every cell's contents tripled, every nerve surrounded.

The bubble in his vein grew, stretched, thinned.

We looked at each other, one by one and all at once.

The moon shone through the window.

We felt like howling. We three, Maude and Abigail and I, my friends, my kin, my selves, multiplied.

So we did.

WE'RE GONNA DIE

1.

LOOK AT ME, SAYS THE BOG MAN TO THE AMERICAN TOURIST. The voice is the rasp of a wind instrument, the scratch of emphysema, the whisper of lungs and larynx dusty with disuse.

The American tourist sits in a Dublin museum, on a metal bench made to look like ancient wood. Her brain thumps and thrashes against her skull.

The Clonycavan man, the display reads. He died two thousand three hundred years ago, an axe to the head. Peat cutters unearthed him by accident deep in the bog, slicing off everything below the belt in the process. But the Irish swamps preserved the idea of him, if not the entirety.

Here lies a man, the American tourist thinks. Not just bones, like the skeletons in the museum's other rooms. Not just things made, daggers and brooches and bowls displayed behind glass her fingers can smudge.

It is mid-morning on a Saturday in June, 2016. The American tourist has been electricity in flight all week for work, gaining and losing time like pounds on a scale during a bender: Chicago to Miami, then New York, then San Diego. Now the American tourist has lost eight more hours during an overnight flight to Dublin, hours taken as if some troll in the air has exacted a price for crossing his drawbridge. Trolls and fairies and spirits. Chicago has its Irish Catholics that play bagpipes at their weddings and funerals, and drink Guinness and Jameson on principle. But the real Ireland. That's the goal.

The American tourist, adrenalized, has been in motion all morning, following narrow streets that refuse to run straight, streets that curve and wind and change names to suit a mood, crossing these streets like a child, looking right and left before sprinting across, still unsure where the traffic will come from, ducking under awnings during every hourly rain, rubbing cold and damp hands.

This museum is Dublin's ode to things buried and discovered. Her brain has unhitched itself from the bone trapping, wobbling and sliding from wall to wall like a torso tossed side to side in the Scrambler ride. Walking intensifies the effect.

Look at me, the bog man says.

So many sleepers here, she thinks, swallowed in their slumber and spit out in foreign times.

Look.

She looks. He has a torso still, but not much else. His head is wrenched to the side, eyes squeezed out. His arms are coiled and frayed like leather braids. His hair is held and preserved by a resin gel, made Irish red by dirt.

Look at them, he says. She looks. College students pose beside the Clonycavan Man's glass box, mouths
open, smiles wide, fingers up in gang signs learned from movies. A mother with tight thin lips drags her sniffling elementary-aged son to the corner, whispers angry words in German. A short red-faced man nearing retirement age studies the bog man from head to chest, adjusts his overstuffed backpack, checks his thick sports watch, and moves on, squeaking in open-toe sandals.

Look at this place, the Clonycavan Man says. *Our tools for eating. Our weapons for killing. Our stones for marking. That's all that's left?*

Was there more? The American tourist whispers to herself.

He laughs. She imagines it like an earthquake, the land that swallowed him opening again. She pictures a wheezing cloud of dust surrounding him, dried bones of plants and animals sucked over centuries into the quagmire.

Were you surprised? The hours lost on the plane seem a theft, a chunk of squishy matter missing from her brain. It feels like a thousand years. He had lost two thousand.

I believed in life after death, he says. *This is different.*

You've become famous, she says as an offering.

Look, he says. She looks. The young boys and old

men and young girls and old women file in and out on a timed march, consulting their guidebooks and lists and notes. With a swift efficient glance, they each mark the Clonycavan Man's dirt-brown color, the ancient hair-style, the texture of rubber skin. They nod, satisfied. They are different. They will never be displayed under glass like meat. Their tools and weapons and stones will never fade or grow blunt. They will matter. They march out, on to the next display.

What was it like? She asks.

Death? Quick, he says. *And slow at once. I felt the axe crack bone.*

No. She breathes it. *Being buried.*

I knew nothing and everything. You lived. I was underneath.

She thinks of the minutes ticking by, minutes to kill until she can sleep, minutes to fill with experience. Only three days here, the limit of time she could wrest away from her anorexic vacation allotment. Time is limited, but it is also too long.

I loved too, the Clonycavan Man says.

Futile to ask him how he knew about her. Futile to pretend she isn't wanting someone, or isn't despairing at not finding someone by thirty, or isn't haunted by the stereotype of women dying alone in sweatpants and cat fur. So she carries on, as if they sit across from each other in a café, or a bar. *What happened?*

He laughs again. It ricochets against his clear coffin. *Nothing left to show under glass.*

She stands on wobbly legs. Her purse has a travel-sized Advil pack, and she dry swallows three.

Magic beans won't help, the Man says.

My head hurts, and this will help. That's the world we live in.

Sorcery. That's nothing new.

My head hurts because I flew here today, from a place you never knew. That's our world. It's better than yours.

He's quiet a moment. *I traveled,* he says. *I saw things in the vast green and blue. And when I returned to my home, I felt different. I did not settle back into my life in the same way.*

She nods politely, as she would in a café, or a bar. The novelty of the moment and experience gone. *Time to go,* she says. She waves, an out-of-place gesture like something in a dream.

Look underneath, he says as she goes out into the light.

2.

We were playing on the street, the tenement children say.

The American tourist scrutinizes the picture, tries to see the humans under the monochrome. The tenements, the tour guide says, were the worst in pre-WWI Europe. A child mortality rate of near half.

There was a man, the kids say. *A smart bow and vest under his suit.*

The American tourist has had coffee, along with a cheddar toastie at a slim slip of a café on the River Liffey. The food and coffee eased her head's pain, perking her up to push on. She picked among the next options: church foundations left from Viking invaders, castles built piecemeal by English invaders, beer and whisky factories built by Irish subjects. She settled on a museum near her hotel, billed for tiny size and maximum impact. Authenticity, with artifacts donated by citizens. The real Ireland.

In the picture the small human faces show suspicion and excitement at once. She imagines they learned both early in the Dublin of a century past.

He had a machine around his neck, they tell her.

The tour guide, a puckish figure with pointed beard and platform loafers, talks the group through photos and documents pasted end to end onto the Georgian row house walls. As he speaks to the dozen Americans and Canadians and Brits and Scots he seems to grow taller than his natural leprechaun stature. He drops his voice over the glassed diaries of young girls beaten by the Magdalenes, raises his voice next to the framed list of Sinn Fein rebels and a tattered flag of the Republic.

Standing before the photograph, taken around the time Dublin declared independence from the Brits in 1916, the guide describes how the Liffey cut the city into have and have not, ghettos on the

north and mansions, like this museum's home, on the south. He describes the truism of any society — the poor bear the biggest burden in war, and in revolution.

The guide moves on, to a real Victrola, to newspapers from the 1910s, then into the next room dedicated to U2. The American tourist stays at the photograph.

The man said his machine could capture our image in time.

Her head bobs and weaves, a punch-drunk shadow boxer. Here in this room are more sleepers, people under glass, beneath the floorboards, underground.

He bade us get our mothers, the kids say.

So we got our Ma from upstairs of our building. A small woman she was. Her sharp bones fought through her skin, made her look stretched and tight from face to feet. She had hair the color of her skin. She was pregnant again.

Our Ma said, What's this now? Down and up she looked the man in his fine clothes, his thick black hair, his uncracked face, his straight back.

The man with the machine said he wanted to photograph as many of the tenement dwellers as possible, to take down names and facts, to take pictures inside the homes. He said, We want to show the leaders in Dublin Castle who you are.

Ma pulled herself up tall as she could and she said, Who I am? I'm living here, aren't I? She pointed up toward our room on the fourth, and then to the crowd on the stones.

The man said, I mean no harm. My organization, we try to help, by showing the conditions in which you live.

Ma surprised us. We expected her to rage. But instead, she stepped back and held a hand out. Then please, she said, do come in.

We all clambered behind them, a line of us children snaking up the building's stairs. Ma said, the conditions in which we live. You'll see the conditions. But first mark these stairs. You'll count 46 before we're through. I collect our water every day from the courtyard well, the single well, mind you, and carry the full buckets up these 46 stairs. I don't look like much, but no one else to do it.

The man said, Your husband?

Ma kept climbing, and we followed. Ma said, Killed his first week in France. Same week I learned I was having another of them. She pointed to us, to all of us.

The man shook his head.

Say what you will about those English in the Castle, Ma said, at least they gave us something.

The man said, Do you not support independence? We children thrilled at the sound of this word. On the street we'd been hearing all sorts about the fight and the rebellion.

Ma stopped on our floor and turned back. She said, The men talking of the great Ireland, the evil occupiers? How does talk feed all them?

The man reached the landing, breathing hard. We thought the machine he carried must weigh much, or perhaps he was too rich to walk stairs often.

Ma stood at our room's door and said, Won't you come in?

The man moved to the center of the room, and we crowded round. He turned, looking at the bed, the table, the floor, the walls. He said, How many are you?

Ma said, six now. Seven soon.

He said, All in this one room? The man looked hard at our bed, and the table, the walls, and we looked at them in turn.

Ma said, And consider all who live here. Not just the six living, no. There's the children's father, of course, dead but still a presence. And the other children. I've borne twelve in all. Two babies that died before taking breath or name. But four others. Children. Baptized and christened. They made words before they died. Made me smile. All before dying. They all live here too.

The man fiddled with his machine and said, It's disgraceful, what they've done.

Ma got sharp and tall and said, Who's that now?

The man said, The men in power, who take all the money for themselves.

And you give all yours away, do you?

The machine made a brilliant noise and a light

flared. We children gasped and clapped.

The man said, I will tell them about you.

Yes, Ma said. Tell them about the stairs and the dead and the living. And the filth. Tell them how we use the water I haul to clean, but the dirt's so deep, on ourselves, in this room, it never yields.

We looked around again, wishing to see what the man did, what Ma talked of. The walls were pocked, yes. And yes, there was a dark color to them. And yes, the floor was covered in mud and the bed crawling with nits and the air smelled of dirt we wore and the filth we put out and the hallways were lined with it and the other rooms full of families dead and living. But what else was there?

The man took a few more photographs, as he called them, in our room and out in the hall, his nose curled.

After a time, we all trudged back to the courtyard, and the man lined us up. He bade us stay still, and photographed us. It was a curious feeling, like our skin crawling, as the machine did its magic to capture us. We wondered would some part of us be stuck in that machine forever?

The man took down names from each of the mothers, who had come out to see the ruckus. He came to Ma last. On his paper, he wrote how many children she'd had, how many died, and had her sign her name.

Ma asked, that's it? The man nodded, and Ma shook her head, and rubbed her belly from where our sister would come weeks later. She'd mewl and cry a few months, keeping us all awake in our bed, then die. Ma'd be alone with us a few years, hauling her water and collecting her widow's money and curling around us children in our bed. Then she'd send us away, to America and Australia and Canada.

But in front of the man with the photograph machine and lists of Irish poor and dead, she rubbed her belly. She said, You've got the touch of some spirit. Who I am, who we are, doesn't matter. You know that well as I.

The man said, But it will.

Ma said, I'm a mother and a wife. I breathe and eat and sleep and shit. I make babies. Then I'll die.

The man looked at us then, a look to his mouth like he might sick up. We felt who we were.

Ma said, But you do what you will. Go back to your many rooms and your notions. Leave us rats to squeak and crawl.

We children watched the man go, and watched Ma climb back up the stairs.

In the museum, the American tourist sees Ma and the man and the children go as if from under glass. She backs away, out of the room, with its sleepers and shadows, out of the tight row house and into the weak Irish sun.

3.

I'm still alive, the American tourist says, to herself, to Dublin.

After the museums, she wanders, drunk on time. She

chooses a pub that advertises a fish and chips deal. Her fellow eaters are Americans and Canadians and Dutch and French. Her food is cardboard, her beer water.

She wanders again, following the curving streets. It's Saturday night, nearing eight, and crowds are starting to gather around doorways leading to lights and thumps. There's a quiet curve she makes, and a tiny pub tucked in the corner. Just like the best bars, the crappy ones, the live ones, back home. The real Chicago.

Inside, the bar stretches long, the tables low to the ground and the stools lower. Men occupy all the seats, and stand where there are none. A man plays guitar in the far back, and a few capped men her father's age line booths nearby and sing along.

She orders Harp, two in one go. She drinks the first fast and sips the second. Her head is cotton bulbs, no longer servant to gravity.

Men are looking at her in this bar. Two Harps in, she wonders what it would be like to take a stranger back to her hotel.

She orders her third beer, and the man standing next to her says hello. He asks if she's waiting for someone. Here we go, she thinks, noting his white-blonde hair (too bad he's not ginger), his height equal to hers (too bad he's not the kind that could throw her around), his age (too bad he's at least ten years older).

It's just no one comes here alone, he says. Women, I mean.

There's no mistaking the pity. She drinks her Harp fast. Her head is no longer filled with fluff, but gradually emptying. She grabs the wood lip of the bar.

The life around her is morphing, along with the bright evening light. The men that fill the bar seem frozen, pinioned under glass like specimens. The American tourist stumbles, her knees failing her. The Irish man holds out a hand. She slaps it away, and strides out of the bar into the street.

Around another corner, she finds a church, tall and steepled in the way of Europe, architecture striving to reach heaven. She knows there's no heaven to reach, knows that the men guarding this church may have scarred altar boys and parish kids under the word of their god. She still admires the gusto that built these structures, the bombastic way they declared themselves holy, an appreciation perhaps purely American.

Behind the church is a patch of graves, scattered and tossed like an unruly vegetable garden. There are monuments, marble angels and crosses and dour portraits for those who could afford it, small stones for those who could not.

I'm still alive, they say, the rotted corpses under the American tourist's feet.

Her head spins in the way that she sometimes seeks at home, the way that erases rational thought and lets her simply exist, dance, drink, eat. Do what her body wants, without judgment. But without those stolen hours grounding her muscle and bone, the spinning is making her guts roil and spasm. She sinks down in the grass, as the June sun finally fades.

Let us out, they say. *We're buried here.*

The American tourist grips the grass, wills her stomach to stay in place and her brain to stop its jostling.

It was all lies, they say. *There's nothing else down here.*

She sees them, men in wool work pants and caps, women in long skirts and sensible sleeved shirts. She sees the others, men in breeches and boots, ties and coats, women in bodices and bouffants. They tell her their names, names that disappear in the same instant from their lips, from her ears. They tell her their stories, lives that meld together and erase themselves while they're told.

There's nothing else, they say, the poor men and women with resignation, the rich with horror.

The American tourist spins and spins, and the sun has gone down and the shadows come out, growing like spores on the graves, and the buried people are close, too close, eyes to her eyes, noses touching, their hands on her arms.

There's nothing, they say, and she hears it in her ears and chest. A deep rumble of anger like thunder. *There's no one,* they say, and she sees them cease to be men and women and rich and poor. They've merged, cast off their clothes, cut off their birthmarks and hair and fingerprints, become one monstrous shape. She cries, the American tourist, because she recognizes this shape, because it's followed her here, through the lost hours, crawling its way back into and under her skin.

Only dirt, it says.

4.

The American tourist wakes again on the street, stumbles into a cab, finds her hotel.

Her bed is clean, crisp, white. She sleeps well past her phone alarm and into the next afternoon.

For the first time in months, she does not dream the dream that makes her sweat through her nightshirt, the dream she never remembers, the dream that makes her mewl and cry in the bed like a dying newborn. She doesn't dream, and when she wakes she feels buoyant from that lack. She feels real. The real me, she thinks.

5.

The American tourist spends the next two days certain of life's facts, certain of where she is, and where she is not.

She visits wide parks with glaring green and twee footbridges over the River Liffey, statues of pompous James Joyce and flaming Oscar Wilde. She eats burgers and drinks Guinness. She takes a bus to Glendalough, a secluded monastery, and spends hours walking through graves, reminding herself of her certainties.

She flies back to Chicago, and her lost hours return. She drags their weight through the airport and the L ride home. She collapses under their weight onto the faux-leather loveseat in her tiny apartment and watches old episodes of *Buffy the Vampire Slayer* fighting the undead in cemeteries, making herself stay awake until the clock declares it bedtime. She buys groceries the next day in the haze of the extra hours, returning home with sacks filled with sweets, like a child left on her own.

Eventually, the American tourist reabsorbs the hours. They warp and expand her a bit, puzzle pieces left in a molding basement. She slips back into her life, with her edges sharper and cut at different angles. At the worst moments, her new contours feel gritty, like dirt. She thinks her eyes tell lies, her heart gives phantom beats. But in the good moments, her new shape feels vast and mysterious, like the dust from stars.

BULL IN THE HEATHER

Transcriber note: *Immediately after the multiple live streams, Aurelia Borgan's election video was banned by the Committee. However, I found an audio recording of the video, buried deep under wires. I had a few minutes before it too was erased. This transcription is based on that recording. Select notes are included for context.*
—*FemmSolo23*

{Clapping; classical guitar music}
Thank you, everyone! Thank you for coming!
{Cries of *Bor-gan* as the music fades}
Leslieanna, I told you I'd play classical![1]
{Laughter; the music boosts in volume for twelve more seconds; clapping on the downbeats}
Betting on the bull in heather! Ha!
{Music fades}
I promised, didn't I? I promised to run this campaign

---

[1] This selection was created by a twenty-first century grouping of musicians who called themselves Sonic Youth. The band featured a married couple, and the group disbanded when the couple divorced. Soon after the Life Elections were instituted, the female was named a Solo past expiration.

my way, and run my election night the same. Oh stop cringing, Patrick! It's good music, even if it's old!

{Boos and laughter}

All right, all right.

{Sound dies down}

Well. Here we are, at the end of a long year and a hard-fought campaign. As you know, the results will be coming in soon.

{Chanting in sync: *Bor-gan, Bor-gan*}

Thank you! But boy, hasn't 2085 been a long year? My goodness. I feel like I've aged a decade in the last twelve months!

{Shout: *2086 will be better!*}

Let's hope that's true, and I can see the year turn, right?

{Clapping; cheers}

But seriously. Down to business, and why we're all here.

I'm confident I've made my case for this year's elections. Now, of course, it's up to the voters.

We've got a few minutes left before the results are in. And then you'll see if you win too, won't you? Right, Tiernan? How many coins did you put on me to win?

{Laughing}

Or to lose? I know you! You too, Patrick! Hedging your bets. I've been there, I get it!

{A loud laugh; a *whoo*}

Anyway. Before the results do come in, a quick word of thanks. Every one of you had the option to shun me.

You had every right to focus on your families and children, and leave a Solo like me to the fates. You also had every right to down-vote me, and urge your networks to do the same. You would have been protecting yourselves and your kin from my influence.

But you didn't. I thank you from the bottom of my heart, as the olds used to say.

And not only that, some of you went further, gifting valuable resources! Thank you Maryella, who donated this room to us for the next hour!

{Clapping}

Such a generous gift. Maryella owns this house, and rents her rooms by the hour to contract workers. So she's giving up tenant coin for this moment. Thank you.

Plus: I hope you're all enjoying the soy bites and extra ration of spring water. That's thanks to Leslieanna. Some of you know she's a chef at my training center. Her grease balls always make the kids smile!

And that's not all. I have a surprise for you! Tiernan, can you pass around the liquid tubes? Make sure everyone gets one.

{Indistinct noises; shuffling}

Don't make that face, Maryella, it's supposed to be black! Everyone, raise your tube. As the ancient Irish used to say, *Slant-a!* Cheers! To you!

{Laughs and coughs}

Good, right? They used to call this *soda*. I found a trove of aluminum cans in my foster father's bunker.

Patrick, can you believe your father had this? The
bubbles are something, aren't they!

Enjoy this treat, everyone.

And while you do, I want to talk about this
extraordinary campaign.

Think about the odds for a minute. I announced my
run for the Life Election last year. A nice coincidence
that the New Year's Eve deadline was also my birthday,
eh? So I announced on the day I turned forty-four.
Right at the last minute.

Did you all think I was going to cede the election
option? Just live out my last year, and give myself up at
forty-five? I considered it. I really did.

You know why? I'll be very honest with you, as I've
tried to be from the start of this campaign. I couldn't
afford the life marketing companies and the life
producers that the winning candidates usually have.
And if I could, I would have needed to start when I was
in my thirties, give them plenty of time to create the
compelling kind of election documentaries and films.

And even if I'd skipped those, most other winning
candidates know how to dance or sing, or do some sort
of flashy talent show. Something to show their bodies
and pretty faces, all the things that are valuable and
worth giving resources to. Again, nothing I had and
nothing I could do.

As most of you know, I've been a contract teacher
since graduating public college, so something truly
winnable just wasn't possible.

So I waited, the deadline looming. I'm not sure what ultimately pushed me towards running in the election. But I finally did, minutes before the new year.

I announced my run, not in a flashy pad ad like most, but with a simple post note. I was one of thousands, in a sea of nobodies. Just think about how many people run for Life Election every year. All the Solo women. All the Crippled. All the Darks.

And then, something strange happened. Out of the clutter of posts, across all the feeds, somehow I got attention. People began spreading me into further and further networks. Until I finally became one of the top races for this year. Me! A Solo from Des Moines, Iowa.

{Clapping}

You know, I've thought a lot about why people reacted to me over others. Why I gained attention.

I was ashamed of my short post note at first. That's the truth. Think about all it had going against it!

In fact. We should remind ourselves of where we started. Take a look at that note. Yes?

{Cheering}

Patrick, can you cue up the clip?

{Clapping}

{Shuffling; a loud pop as the speakers start}[2]

View opens on a bare beige wall, the standard found in contract tenant housing. After three seconds, Aurelia

---

[2] For this section, I include the audio, as well as description of the video. For visuals, I consulted the original announcement post, which still lives on the wires.

Borgan comes into view and sits on an unseen cushion.
The vid AI reader scrolls the scan:

> Status: Solo
> Age: 44
> Category: Plain
> Contract: -39 [3]

After four more seconds of adjustment, she speaks:

*Hello. My name is Aurelia Borgan. I'm forty-four years old,
and I'm running for the Life Election. I don't have any
videos, or props, or talents, or skin to show. I have my
original face. My hair is turning gray. I have never tried to
have a child, so I have no empty nursery. I am a woman
who's unmarried and childless and will soon turn the
expiration age. I ask to live. I deserve to live. That is all.*

Aurelia stays in view for sixty additional seconds. She does
not smile, or cry. At the end of that minute, she rises, and
the vid stops soon after.

{Shuffling; the speakers turn off. Groans}
The next morning I was mortified. I almost deleted
that post note. Can you believe how straight I spoke?
I'd actually nearly questioned the law!
{Silence for several seconds}
Listen to me, I'm getting wound up. I still can't
believe I wasn't snatched up immediately.

---

[3] Corresponds to the number of years left in her federal work
contract. Aurelia was contracted to the Shady Way Training
Center for Youths.

But something about that straightness and honesty appealed. The next morning I found I was at the top of the election rankings for Iowa. By the end of the month, I'd topped Midwest races.[4]

Maybe people were laughing at me, or pitying me, as they voted me up. I did think about that.

But you know, I chose to believe that my popularity was more than just pity or punishment. I like to think my campaign is speaking to people for other reasons, that others sometimes question why we have to run for our lives.

Oh boy! There go your pads. Recording this. More straight talk will liven up your feeds, eh?

I best give you something valuable then!

{Laughs}

So like I was saying. I understand there's the drain on resources. I understand that the Committee had to make hard decisions when it formed so long ago, when our ban on exported people and products meant not enough food for everyone. And Solos simply didn't contribute to the Future of Glory. None of the undesirable groups did.

I understand. And for a long time, I watched the Life Elections like everyone else. I placed bets on the most pathetic Solos, and the most compelling Darks. I even

---

[4] Throughout the year, Aurelia moved up and down in the rankings of top contenders, peaking at #3 Most Desired to Live in the Midwest region.

bet on the Solo men contests.[5] It was primo enter-
tainment! And I was good at it, often winning our
yearly bracket pool at work. I never pictured myself as
a candidate, even knowing I was a bastard child from a
Mongrel union. I thought my removal from my proto-
family and placement with my foster family would set
me up for a real shot.[6] I'd get ahead of my expenses,
finish up my service term, find a mate, prove my worth.
As all of you have.

But as I grew older and that didn't happen, I stopped
making bets. And now—

{A shout: *It's here*}

Oh!

{Shuffling; what is most likely the crowd parting for
the Committee messenger}

It's time.

{Indistinct murmurs and chatter}

I've just been handed the final results in a live note.
Once I tap this sheet, we'll know.

The New Year's artillery barrage will start in a
couple minutes, and then...

I'm, well, I'm feeling good, how about you?

{Clapping, growing in volume and speed}

All right, yeah! Thank you!

---

[5] At the time of this recording, male Solos were still required to
cede their lives or run for Life Election at age 75. The
requirement for males has since been eradicated.
[6] Refers to the informal start of re-placement. This later codified
into our current system, whereby Darks and Mongrel children
who score 99% on placement tests in elementary school are
awarded new white families. They must still run for Life Election
at age thirty; but more resources are at their disposal.

{Chanting and stomping for one hundred and
fourteen seconds: *Bor-gan, Bor-gan*}

It's time: let's count down!

{Crowd joins Aurelia in her counting}

10! 9! 8! 7! 6!

Whew, I'm shaking!

5! 4! 3!

Almost there!

2!

Ah!

1!

{Distant sounds of the annual federal mortars,
cannons, and grenades as the clock hits twenty-four}

And...

{Sounds of celebratory artillery from locals outside;
handhelds, assault rifles, and pipe bombs can be
discerned}

Here it comes! Here's what it says!

{Aurelia reads from live note:}

*The People have voted, and Aurelia Borgan has lost her
Life Election.*

{A groan, cut off quickly. Silence, lasting twenty-
two seconds. Coughs and indistinct sounds}

Well.

That...

Wait, there's more now. *At forty-five years of age, she
has not presented sufficient or compelling reason to continue.*

{Indistinct murmurs and chatter, lasting thirty-six
seconds}

Could I get some water?

{Shuffling}

Just a moment, please.

Wow. I really, really didn't...

{A shout: *when?*}

What? Oh. When. Yes. Let me...

The Committee for Life Reassessment and Redistribution recognizes the will of the People. Due to egregious slander, the Committee has waived the regular waiting period of one week, and decreed the Life Redistribution will be completed immediately.

{Groans, a gasp}

Yes. Yes. OK.

Well.

I can see, yes, the live note does not lie: Our numbers are already growing.

{Doors opening, shuffling. A low male voice: *Aurelia Borgan, the Committee demands you come with us for your sentence*}

Here are our Life Protectors, coming to protect all of you. Yes.

{Shuffling; the sound of LPs charging their generators}

Don't worry, Tiernan, Maryella, all of you. You're all safe. You've got your families, after all. You work free and clear. You own things.

Excuse me. Just a bit more water. It's quite hot in here, isn't it?

{Silence, lasting sixteen seconds}

I'm glad you're all still recording. Are you seeing this too? How the colors are suddenly brighter? Maybe that's my eyes playing tricks. One last burst of vision.

{Silence, lasting seven seconds}

Yes, recording still. Wouldn't want to miss a lost election, would you? I'm sure you'll see your feed scores rise when people find out you were here. You can coast off this for a while. Maybe I would too.

Yes. I...yes.

Life Redistribution. Do the words sound funny to you?

{A shout: *Recount*}

That's nice. Yes. A nice thought.

Did you know? That used to be something that happened.

{Sound: might be flapping of her hands, as one does on extreme heat warning days}

I just remembered. When I was in school, because that's what it was called then, not training centers. I found an old history book. It was one of those books that hadn't been cleaned. Did you know elections used to be for something else? They used to be for officials. Committee members. Leaders, even, though they went by something else. Presidents, I think. Hard to imagine, right? I think, if I remember right, our Leader actually started out that way. He was elected.[7]

Elections weren't for regular people. Not even for

---

[7] Unconfirmed, but a well-known rumor on the wires. Since our Leaders cede their birth names upon ascension, we don't know who Aurelia might refer to. But many suspect this occurred around the time of the Great Cleanse of 2027 in the European territories.

women like me, or Cripples, or Darks. Imagine that. People didn't have to justify their lives.

{Shuffling}

That's what I was doing, you know.

{Silence for nine seconds}

As much as my vid didn't follow the mold, I was still trying to justify who I was.

{The LPs: *Aurelia Borgan, you are commanded to—*}

And I still lost. It was full of lies, and still.

{The LPs: *Turn around and put out your wrists*}

I see you, Life Protectors. No one can miss those red uniforms. So red. Garish, really. And yes, your weapons. So shiny, and black. Can't miss those.

{The LPs: *Turn around—*}

I know, I know.

Don't worry, I'm not going to run. No reason not to admit it now. I didn't want to do our national duty, my duty. I never did, even though it's evil not to.

I'm still alive. I feel so alive.

And you can't show that ending, can you? You can't live stream Life Redistribution, right?

{Shuffling; speaker moving around the room as she talks}

I lied in that vid, and I lost, so why lie anymore? Why not say words I told myself I could never say aloud? Words that stop up my mouth sometimes, they're so keen on getting out?

{Rustling, shouts}

Maybe that's why I ran for the Election. I wanted to

tell you all. I'm glad. I'm glad I didn't get married. Because I didn't want to be owned.

{Gasps}

Ha! You know, you think words so long in your head, and push them aside again and again, but still they come. And you tell yourself that you can never say them out loud, even though they want to be said.

{Crash; probably a thrown tube}

Ooo, look how the Life Protectors are tensing up.

Did you know LPs are contract? I learned that somewhere.

Contract. You know that old history book? It described contract workers like us. We're indentured servants. Born poor, offered a deal, coin that's spent before it's made. And we'll never reach the end of our term. I'll never stop training those goddamn youths.

But we can't admit that. If we just worked harder, just played the game, put in our time. We'd be full citizens. We'd be owners of things. Right?

{Beeps of LP radios}

I feel the blood pumping in my wrists and neck right now. Where will that go? And how...how will it happen?

{Shuffling}

Do they gas us? Shoot us? You never see anything after elections. Even for those lucky few, the ones that bow and scrape enough to win a few years more. We don't see the winners after elections either, do we?

{A shout: *Aurelia, we'll—*}

Shut up. All of you.

And yes, here are your pad cameras. You all won't look at me with your eyes, hmm? Have to see this on your screen? That makes sense. Doesn't it, Les?

Leslieanna?

{Quieter}

Remember? I don't want to lie anymore. Please, let's not, OK? Remember that night and what we did? How we tasted, and—

{Shout, probably from Leslieanna: *Liar*}

Les, don't leave. No, don't, I need you, please!

{Booing; doors slamming}

No.

No, I won't go.

{Thumps, objects hitting the floor or speaker}

I won't.

{LPs: *Aurelia Borgan, hold out your wrists*}

I'm just. I'm just going to sit for a while. Here on the floor. OK?

Back off! Just give me a fucking minute.

You'll all get your ending.

{LP beeps; shouts}

They say being alone is so lonely, you know? When I was younger, when I still had plenty of time, my friends would ask, *Why would you be Solo? Aren't you lonely?* I always thought they confused two terms. Loneliness was different than being alone.

{Boos}

Being alone was different. I felt free. Even now.

{Shuffle. Beeps grow louder}

I know. But my blood, it's pumping so fast. Where will it go?

{Silence for eight seconds}

I want you all to see me. Stop recording, will you? Look at me.

{A boo}

Look at me!

If I throw something? Scream and cry? Will you look at me?

{A crash}

There — how about that? All these tubes, these stupid resources?

{Some in the crowd boo, others chant: *Borgan*}

Fuck this. I'm not going, I'm not—

{Rustling, stomping}

Wait—

{The mechanical sound of the Life Cuffs cinching on wrists}

Oh. Oh. Wow.

I always wondered what these felt like. I'd seen them on people on the feeds, after their elections. They looked so cold, all clear and plastic.

But they're warm.

That's strange.

{Clapping, the sound of feet, a clamor of voices}

{Aurelia emits a loud moan}

— END OF RECORDING —

Transcriber note: *According to official Committee records,*

Aurelia Borgan underwent Life Redistribution at 02:56 on the morning of January 1, 2086. By the end of her life term, an equal amount of bets had been placed on her victory and her defeat, bets totaling a record twenty-six million in coin.

After Life Election results every year, applications for marriage licenses always spike. But by January 30, 2086 applications had doubled the past record.

WE USED TO WAIT

WHEN THE MAIL CAME IN SEPTEMBER, IT WAS FROM another man. The post office made Beverly pick it up. She traveled by two trains and a bus to get there, spent the last of her change to pay the missing postage. Afterwards, on the L platform, she tore the envelope's edge with a nail bed turned bloody from picking.

The letter was dated April, before the Germans surrendered. Before thousands more men were thrown across South Pacific jungles and hills like underhand softballs. Before the bomb. Before the other bomb. Before the final Japanese surrender.

On the train north to Foster, Beverly folded the letter again. She wondered whether he intentionally left off the extra stamp, if that was the reason it was delayed, taking months instead of weeks to travel across the sea by ship, across the country by truck, across Chicago by car.

Another version of him had sent the letter, one still alive and hopeful. She received his letter the way she'd received the final telegram: stoic, calm, assuming an air of grace. Searching herself for sadness, and feeling only a slight searing in her palms.

April 2, 1945

Beverly,

We're on another island, can't say where. It's so hot. Back home I bet you still have the blankets on at night. I've forgotten what cold feels like.

And then I remember how cold you are. How frigid. How could you be so cold?

Quinn had lived down the street when they were in school. That's all it took.

Beverly and her mother had a six-flat near Foster, the Rosehill cemetery to the north and Winnemac Park to the south. The park was quiet back then and the cemetery raucous, the teens daring each other to walk across the dead in the dark in order to prove themselves alive. Beverly and her friend Mary did it a few times, Mary always following one boy or another, Beverly following Mary.

One autumn night in 1938 Tom Quinn was there, youngest of the six Quinns that lived in a five-room apartment across from the park. She'd seen his brothers around school, one in every year. Tom was younger than her. Everyone called him Quinn, because he was just a body and they couldn't be bothered to learn another first name.

Later, years later, she would try to remember him at that moment in time. Dots of black across his lip and chin, wisps of whiskers. The black on his head brutally oiled and slicked, with a few strands fighting their way free, standing at attention. His belt was notched at the smallest width, yet his trousers still hung loose. His shoes were Viking ships, so big they pushed him off balance. He was unformed, a body growing unevenly, a person in flux.

The girls carried flasks, their lipstick bloodying the spouts. The boys plucked cigarettes from behind their ears, the white wrappers yellowed with hair grease. They sat near a mausoleum laughing, drinking, smoking.

Tom Quinn stood apart. Beverly caught him looking at her. She looked away, at her bare feet under her skirt, shoes kicked off to feel the dirt and death beneath. She looked back, quick darts. His eyes, black and wide, roamed over her fine blonde bob, her thick nose, her drawn-on lips and eyebrows, her bra boosted with paper padding, her dress that was a little too tight in the waist.

Quinn watched Beverly. Beverly watched Mary.

Mary laughed and drank and smoked most of all. Mary, her breasts bound up like a bouquet in her tight-white shirt, tails tied under her ribcage to show off a freckled midriff that glowed white in the moonlight. Mary, her fat lips colored the red of cartoon devils. Mary, her Dorothy Lamour hair and hips. Mary, her dark brown birthmark smudging the side of her neck, an inexcusable flaw in other girls, an embraced "beauty mark" in her lingo. All the boys watched Mary. All the girls did her bidding. Beverly wanted to be Mary. And she wanted something more, something she couldn't name that involved Mary always, in all states. She wanted to not want this — everything she should want in life was already named.

The worst was when Mary would choose a beau for the month, or week, or night. Some boy or another, thin and open-mouthed, ready with a cigarette or a drink, waiting his turn at those lips and hips.

That night in Rosehill Mary chose a Quinn, the oldest one, two years out of high school, at least five years older than them. He was tall, lanky, black-haired, like Tom. When Mary kissed him, standing next to the stone of the mausoleum, under the light of the moon through the trees, they looked like Adam and Eve, condemning all the others to sin.

Beverly looked again at the youngest Quinn. He had not moved, his body or eyes. She motioned him to her, brought him close, and when she kissed him she imagined a line between them, connecting the brothers, bringing her lips to Mary's.

Why won't you write me, Bev? Should I just let myself be shot? There's plenty that will do it. They're everywhere here, hiding in the trees and the mud. They want to kill us all. Is that what you want?

Beverly's mother seized on the news.

She sat perched on Beverly's twin bed, a cigarette between her thumb and index finger. Like a man. "It doesn't matter if he's a little younger."

"Mother." Beverly was propped against her pillow, working an algebra problem with a newly sharp pencil.

"It doesn't. All those women looking for the older man have it wrong. It's the younger ones that will stay."

Ruth's own husband had run away when Beverly was a baby. One look at a nappy, Ruth said, and he hit the road. When very young, after hearing that story, Beverly took to holding in her movements, bowels clenched until she was so miserable and bloated Ruth put castor oil in her pudding. But Beverly thought the things in her body could drive people away, and kept thinking it, as her colon finally unclenched.

"I'm not seeing Tom Quinn," said Beverly.

"That's not what he says." Ruth smiled. "His mother told me he's talking about you all the time. Even in front of his brothers. And you know boys don't talk love with other boys."

Beverly's guts churned. Under her algebra homework his first letter lay waiting. There was heat to it, threatening to burn through her responsibilities and talents and goals. It would burn her up. *I think of you every moment of every day*, in a tight cramped handwriting of curlicues and capitals, a style that made her think of the girls in her class, of Mary. She'd set it aside, read no more.

"Why don't you have him over for dinner, Bev?"

Beverly shook her head. Mary had cast aside her Quinn. So Beverly had no more use for hers.

Ruth pulled the cigarette from her lips, jabbing it

towards Beverly. "Invite him over. Next Friday. You won't be a tease, Bev. That's the worst a girl could be."

Beverly wanted to object. But this was what she was supposed to do. After all, a boy would turn into a man, and a man would take care of her. This boy seemed like he might be nice, and become a nice man. Beverly felt on the jagged precipice of something, and Quinn was holding out a hand, leaning so far over he might fall.

Ruth pushed herself off the bed, her wide hips popping and thick ankles cracking. Beverly saw her own slightly slimmer hips, her own ankles, and the way both of their chins squared off, the way the hair on their arms grew thick and blonde, the puckered fold of flesh above their knees. This is what she would look like one day. That, and her mother's clean commands, were Beverly's future, laid out. Beverly chafed at knowing what was to come and what she should do. At the same time she silently thanked her mother for the compass.

Cold fish. That's what you are, Bev. It took the heat here to make me see it. This heat makes my sweat run like a tap. I can't control it. I didn't know how much water was in my body, how much I could sweat.

You don't sweat. You don't have enough water in you. You're stone.

There was novelty the first time. A bit of pain, a flicker of something down there and in her chest. Her mother left for cigarettes and a long walk. Beverly watched

Quinn take his clothes off, hunched over, trembling, in her bedroom. She felt something then, watching him. She took off her own clothes, standing straight and steady. He leaped at her, pushed her to the bed, a flurry of kisses brushing her lips, her chin, her nipples, her belly button. He thrust a finger in the direction of where she bled, probing through folds of tissue as foreign to her as him. Then he pushed his penis in. She breathed hard for his minute of grunting, thinking of other pains she had managed in the past: a shot in the arm at the doctor's office, a broken toe when she was twelve, watching Mary kiss all her beaus.

He held her afterwards, after he pulled out of her, spilling a sticky warmth on her belly, after he'd wiped it off with a tissue, telling her what they'd just done wasn't a sin. He planned to marry her once they were old enough. Just another year or two, and he'd get a job, buy them a house. They'd be careful until then, he said. He'd keep pulling out of her in time. That's how you made sure no babies came.

Quinn petted her hair, told her not to cry, even though she wasn't crying. He held her and told her he loved her. She let him do all these things, smiled at him when he snuck out of the apartment on tiptoe, smiled at her mother's triumphant hug and offer of ice, smiled. In bed, the sheet's sticky, tapioca colored cream mixing with her tiny bit of rusty blood, she touched herself, where he had punched in. Such a strange way to make a woman, she thought.

Afterwards, every time they did it, her mother in the

other room with the radio loud, she closed her eyes and let him kiss her, fuck her, hold her, love her. She smiled, breathed as he did, repeated his words back to him.

You know what I miss, Bev? Driving. We don't drive here. We're driven places, shipped places. More often than not we walk. Or run. We run a lot. Towards things, away from things. Things that I'd tell you about if you cared. I'm scared of the things we run towards. There's the Jap snipers, and the Jap pilots that use their planes as bombs to blow carriers off the bay. There's nowhere to run to, really — we're on a fucking island, surrounded by more islands with people that look like Japs.

But we keep running, and keep getting driven and shipped places, all of them hot, wet. I want to drive in snow.

They married, of course, once they were both out of high school. There was nothing else to do. A couple of Beverly's male classmates went on to the university in Champaign. A handful of his class went on to teacher training and trade school. But neither of them had the money for that.

Quinn joined the union, learned about pipes and how to clean them. She worked the counter at a drug store on Argyle.

He wore his father's suit and she her mother's dress to the courthouse in the Loop. His brother joined them as witness, the brother Mary had kissed. Beverly looked down the halls for Mary, even though she'd moved away right after graduation. Mary sent her postcards from different states, sparely written, announcing marriage, then divorce, then new men. All signed off with Xs and Os. Beverly kept them in a box under the bed.

Quinn and Beverly signed papers, joked they'd always be able to do the anniversary math, wedding in the nice round number of 1940. They splurged on steak at George's on the river. They hugged the older Quinn goodbye, and Beverly fought the urge to kiss him, to feel the ghost of Mary's devil-red lips.

That night, in her room, in the bed where they'd seen each other naked for years, nothing felt different. They would rent a place soon, Quinn promised. Just a brief wait. In the meantime, he said with his eyes down, they could lay as man and wife. She learned that meant seeing his face contort while he was still inside her. She thought of the box of postcards stowed beneath them.

Beverly watched Quinn sleep that night. He lay like a corpse, his arms and legs spread across the bed, mouth open to his molars, belly and penis and soft, fleshy spots unprotected. He was sweet, and kind, and pretty. He was hers. He was the face she would see every morning and every day and every night. He loved her and would never leave her. That was something.

· · ·

That's why you hate me, isn't it, Bev? Because I left to fight?
What would you have me do? Be shamed by everyone for not
going? Run away?

You'd still hate me, though. Why? Haven't I been good to
you? I've told you how much I love you. Other men don't do
that with their wives. You hold my heart. It beats for you.
You're its master.

Tell me what my heart should do now.

On the day after the bombing in Hawaii, the day the
country declared war against Japan, Beverly stopped for
groceries on the way home from work, at the new
corner store a few blocks from their apartment. Their
building was in the curve, where their street trans-
formed into Damen. Their living room looked out on
the Rosehill cemetery. It was cheaper because of the
view. If Beverly squinted, she could see the mausoleum
from that first night they kissed.

She found herself in front of the meat counter and
didn't remember how she'd got there. There was a
haziness to the last forty-eight hours. She was
underwater.

"Beverly?"

As she located the voice behind her, the basket
slipped from her grasp, and she heard Mary's laughter
— the same soft wet laughter as years ago — and then
saw Mary bending to pick up a tin of beans that had
rolled to her feet.

Then they were facing each other, the two of them,

next to a shelf of beans, and Beverly felt their reunion as if viewed from a camera lens. Two people, both from the same neighborhood, both newly 20, both the same gender, the same species. But Mary was bright blue dress, bright red nails and lips, bright white shoes. She held her tongue to the gap in her front teeth, as if the words she would utter were too scandalous to let out. Beverly was beige dress, yellow nails, gray shoes, slack bob and wider hips and smaller chest.

"How long has it been?"

Two years and five months and twenty-four days, Beverly almost said. Instead she shook her head and shrugged.

"You never wrote me back, Bev," Mary said, quiet, a gentle poke to her shoulders. Beverly stayed mute, but marveled at the idea. What would she have said in a letter? What could she say?

Mary talked to fill the silence. She lived just west of the city now. Married again, Frank, a man ten years her senior, an executive in the Loop. She was in the neighborhood visiting her mother for the day, seeing the old street. Her voice was a bit breathy and low, more than it had been. Beverly wanted to close her eyes and listen to Mary say words, any words. She wanted to lay her fingers on Mary's throat, feel the words vibrate from her body, the moment of creation saved just for her.

"Frank will sign up, of course," Mary said. She did the thing they would all do, for years and decades to come: recount *the moment*, the instant they learned of the bombings, the place they were, the resolutions made after. Mary had been at home, the radio on as she entertained her sister and her two-year-old nephew. Beverly herself had been listening to the radio while Quinn gripped her shoulder.

Beverly watched Mary's tongue move in her mouth. She looked older, but ripened. Beverly felt herself shrivel again to let her friend shine.

After Beverly's hands started to ache, from holding her basket and holding herself in her own space, Mary stopped talking. She looked Beverly up and down.

"You married your Quinn, right?"

"Yes."

"And he'll enlist, of course. I'm sure all the Quinns will."

In all the rush, the newness, the surreality of the last two days, in which the world had come to their street, somehow Beverly hadn't thought about this. Would Quinn enlist? Yes. He was a man, a steady one, a moral one. He would do this task. She would be left behind.

In the grocery store, in front of Mary, Beverly felt herself sinking to the floor.

In the two years they'd been married, Beverly did what Quinn said, or what her boss said at the counter, or what her mother said at Sunday dinners. But mostly what Quinn said. It didn't hurt to cede control. It was easy to follow a lovingly made map. It felt good, just.

Now, in the grocery, on the grimy wood floor, Mary and the store clerks calling to her — was she OK? Mary here, above her. Beverly's heart beating too fast, her palms damp with sweat. She wanted to faint, to black out: feeling her body come alive again, realizing Quinn would leave her alone. Who would she listen to then?

Was I too good to you, Bev? I hear some of the other guys talk about their girls and wives. They treat them like dolls, or things you'd throw in the trash bin. Did you want that from me?

Quinn left for boot camp, and Beverly waited. She read Quinn's letters when they arrived in their courtyard mailbox, as full of love as ever, written in his curlicues and capitals. Training to kill men with a gun had somehow turned Quinn even softer with a pencil.

She read slowly, made herself linger, willed his words to be digested for sustenance. But from the first, they tasted like spun sugar, sweet and colorful, incapable of sating her need. She missed the warmth of his torso, the touch of his lips on her forehead, the reminder of who she was.

Beverly assembled paper and pencil, envelopes and stamps. At the kitchen table she curled herself around the ingredients for a letter, and she tried repeating his words back to him. But seeing them on paper — the result was worse than candy. As satisfying as dirt or ash.

So she filed Quinn's letters into their own box kept

on her bedside table, and she felt a void growing in her chest.

Beverly wondered later. If Quinn's letters had been different, could she have waited? If she had opened those envelopes and found terse data firm enough to grip, descriptions of the hot desert of the California boot camp, and the men he was meeting from Texas and the Dakotas and Wyoming, or reminders for the government paperwork to complete and Chicago tax bills to pay — if she had found meat and bones in his letters instead of cotton candy, would they have held her steady?

Why do you punish me, Bev? What did I do?

And then Mary called.

On a Saturday in May, Beverly sat at Mary's kitchen table in her grand Oak Park Victorian, drinking coffee and watching her talk. They'd fallen into their old roles, Beverly coming when called. Mary spoke of the letters she got from Frank, of the ladies down her street collecting old nylons and bits of rubber (and keeping score of who donated most), of the stunning silence of her house. Then she talked of school; dances and pep rallies and boys. How simple it had been.

She cracked a little at that last, water in her eyes. Beverly stared. Mary had always been soft curves, but hard inner lines.

"Remember when we'd walk over the graves?" Mary wiped at the spots that would one day have crow's feet. "It seemed so brave then."

"You were."

"Frank's off being brave. I'll probably go back to that cemetery soon, for his grave."

Beverly felt a lightening then, a relief.

Mary laughed. "You never were one to stop me being scandalous, you know. If I said something like that to the ladies at their rubber drives? Christ."

"It's not scandalous. It's the truth."

Beverly watched the back of Mary's hand, blue veins marking blood paths, as it dabbed at her eyes, then shook on her lap, then lay on the table, inert. Beverly's own hand felt so cold. So she put it on Mary's, and smiled at the heat.

After a moment, Mary turned her hand over, so their palms touched.

They watched their hands, white bones under winter white skin.

"It's shocking," Mary said. "How much you miss touch. When it's gone."

Quinn didn't like holding hands in public, or much at all. Beverly put her fingers in Mary's palm, then twined the two pairs together. The relief came again, a sense of finality.

But Mary pulled away. "The coffee's cold. I'd make more but, you know, rations."

Beverly nodded. Rations. Because of the war. Because of Quinn. She pulled on her jacket.

"So you'll come?" Mary asked. "To the next scrap drive? If you come we can at least make it a laugh."

Beverly nodded automatically, a condition of years of training and instinct.

On a Saturday in June, Beverly placed the latest letter from Quinn into her box, unopened.

From train to streetcar to train, she carried a bag of scraps. Worn clothing and torn nylons and rubber tubing and an aluminum pot. The bag's heaviness on her shoulder a pleasant ache, the valiant pain of action. Trash could be the key to toppling empires, the signs on street corners and billboards said. Waste was the death knell of freedom.

Behind the Lutheran Church of Hope, a tight crowd of people formed clusters surrounding scrap stations. Mary appeared at her elbow. "They'll boast about this for weeks," she said.

Beverly thought of Quinn's open lips and slack face when he slept.

"We mustn't judge, I suppose," Mary said. "It is something to win at." She closed her lips, biting back the rest. Beverly pictured the expanding list of dead marines in the daily *Tribune*.

They moved through the crowd, to the rubber station and stocking station and clothes station and metal station, and removed things from their bags, and walked away lighter. Beverly examined faces at each station. A pregnant woman in her twenties; Beverly imagined a husband on the North African front, a kid brother training on warships. A graying woman with darkness pooling under her eyes; Beverly imagined a husband killed in France in the first war, and two sons training for the invasion of France in this war. A man with no visible limp or excessive age; Beverly imagined a heart condition, and his guilty relief at ineligibility for war. Every person here, sacrificing scraps to the gods of heaven and governments.

After their bags were empty, Beverly followed Mary once again.

They sat at Mary's table, and sipped their coffee slowly to preserve it, and ate their ham sandwiches with small bites. Mary chatted to fill the gaps Beverly left; stories of women in the neighborhood working for the first time, waiting on their stoop for letters, walking freely and unbruised. The sudden absence of men felt fictional, like some alien species or sickness had felled them all, Mary said. It felt like a test of sorts: what would the women do?

"But the men will come back, eventually," Beverly said, surprising herself.

Mary slid her hand across the table, eyes pleading. Beverly twined her fingers with Mary's.

When Beverly returned home, she lay awake in the bed she shared with Quinn. She remembered the ways Quinn touched her in this bed. He pushed himself inside her, yes. But he also delicately brushed his fingers over her nipples, or teased what he said felt like a pearl button between her legs. Or even used his tongue. All of that touching; she'd come to like that part.

And that touching could be done by a man, or a woman. If you closed your eyes, could you even tell? She imagined it: feeling hands on her body, opening her closed eyes and seeing Mary. Her body a brick wall with a gaping hole, and the relief, the shimmering glow of a final piece found.

Mary joined Beverly in the neighborhood one morning in August. They walked through an outdoors market in the park, with vegetables from the farms outside the city, swap stations for tools and repairs, and a stand selling iced treats.

After, at her apartment, Beverly watched Mary assess the small rooms and worn furnishings, all of which could fit into one of Mary's spacious bedrooms. But Mary smiled, cooed at the spindly shelf with small pots of ferns, marveled at the sunny yellow of the walls, gasped at the view. Perfection, Mary insisted.

Once seated at the table, tea and toasted squares consumed over abnormal quiet, Mary held out both of her hands. Beverly added hers. Each time, she heard a latching sound in her head. But this time the sound was a little louder, more jarring. The colors in the room seemed deeper and darker, covered with a burnt amber haze.

"Will you hug me," Mary said, barely a whisper. She stood, still holding Beverly's hands.

Beverly, the essence of who she was, rose out of her body, and that body stayed seated on that seat where she ate dinner with Quinn. This Beverly, standing and facing Mary, she was an idea, a being made entirely of nerve endings and compulsion. This Beverly pulled Mary towards her. She felt the rigid stripes of muscle across Mary's shoulders, and the way they loosened a little under her arms. The skin where Mary's hair hit her neck smelled of cut grass on a humid morning. Beverly kissed that spot, a light touch of her lips. Mary sighed. So Beverly did it again, and again, and moved across her neck, and down.

She stopped then, pearl buttons filling her vision, all other shapes of Mary's body and this room and the world outside concentrated into perfect clear circles. She listened for the direction of sound, and heard Mary's breath, faster than normal.

Beverly worked quick, quicker than Mary's breath, quicker than her own. Thinking required words, and a tether to that numb husk Beverly imagined still sitting at her table. She acted instead.

Mary's breasts tasted like the brine of meat. Beverly held them in her palms, touched them with gentle fingers and rough thumbs. When she looked up she saw Mary's open mouth, Mary's eyes squeezed shut.

Beverly looked down again. The heat of anger colored the pearls and the shirt and the breasts, darker than their vibrant white. Did Mary shut her eyes to think of her husband? Or the boys that had walked over graves? Did she imagine Beverly was someone else, as she felt Beverly reaching down to raise her skirt?

·   ·   ·

That last night, when I was on leave. Almost three years ago now. That's what I've lived with for years. Why?

It was a surprise, that night. He'd been in boot camp in California for a few months, and they'd granted his platoon leave before their deployment. He'd no doubt imagined a triumphant surprise and reunion, tears as he lifted her off the ground, kisses as they ran back to the bedroom.

Beverly was drinking. It was a new habit, two fingers of scotch at night before bed, and sometimes before dinner, and sometimes just during the afternoon on a weekend.

It was barely afternoon, the late summer sun low in the southern sky, its zenith that time of year. Her second scotch of the day was almost gone.

He knocked. He had his own keys, but opted for drama: the swing of the door, the sweep of her feet.

When Beverly opened the door, the sight of the uniform made her chest contract. Still the first year of the war, but the neighborhood was keenly aware of the meaning of uniforms at doors, handing over telegrams.

It's happened, she thought. Her arms went long and tight at her sides. She took a breath, deeper than she had in years, swallowing all the air around her. Her ribs ached, trying to contain this new freedom.

Then she looked at the uniform's face. She shook her head. Stepped back into the apartment. Held her hands out in front of her. Quinn followed. He grabbed her right hand, and she slapped his away. He said her name, again, and she waved her hands over her face and chest, warding him off. Her stomach flipping, she ran to the toilet. She thought she might vomit, she thought she might faint, she thought she might choke around this tightness in her throat, this vice that squeezed and squeezed.

On shaky legs, Beverly ran her hand under the tap. She put the cool, wet, shaking thing on the back of her neck. In the mirror, her face had the gray sheen and deep divots she recognized from her grandmother's wake long ago.

Quinn moved behind her. In the mirror, his face was tanned from the California sun, his black eyes bright, his chest wide and tall. In the cemetery, their first night, he'd reminded her of a corpse come to life, his pasty skin and too-long bones animated by something primal, sexual. Now, readying for killing faraway men, he looked more alive than she'd ever seen.

He smiled, and she stared at his face for a moment.

"I didn't think you'd get this worked up," he said.

Beverly cupped a hand under the faucet and slurped. As she rinsed her mouth, she tried to remember how it was between them. She tried to be happy that she could follow orders again.

"We were all really excited," he said. "To surprise our wives."

"That you did," she said, her voice gravel. She stood, and slipped her arms around his torso. His solid arms curled around her, and she felt a bit of that lightening.

He kissed the top of her head.

He leaned back to look at her and she tried to smile, get hold of her breath.

She crushed herself into his crisp beige shirt again. The initial shock over, she examined their apartment under his arm. The Ficus now sat on the shelves instead of the sill, and the green coverlet from their bed now covered their sofa. Would the shifting reveal how the earth had moved in his absence? And the box of his unopened letters: would that be all she needed to say?

After they pulled apart, and Quinn poured the both of them a glass of scotch, she busied her hands by molding meat into patties. Quinn buzzed with bright energy and words while she worked. When she placed the patty melt in front of him, he tucked in, smiling at her around each bite and sucking his fingers to catch the grease and salt. Quinn told stories of boot camp food, and drills under the searing desert sun. Beverly felt herself, that essence of who she was, slowly sinking back into her mute and numb body, still seated at the table.

When he pushed his plate away, he reached for her hand where it lay in her lap. He spread her palm, and curled his fingers into hers. "I missed this hand."

The feel of another living body touching hers. Mary had said that, how much she'd missed touch, and said it again after she'd shaken and twitched under Beverly's tongue, and again as she rushed out of the house, her clothes reassembled, her curves back in place, her hard lines returned. The last time they'd seen each other.

Quinn brought her knuckles to his lips. "I forgot how you smelled. Like burning leaves."

She closed her eyes. She sent all her senses, all of her intention, towards her hand, willing it to feel something.

"Why didn't you write, Bev?" His voice as soft as it used to be, but with new honed edges.

She shook her head, shrugged.

"Months, Bev. Didn't you miss me?"

Her mouth wouldn't work, even to save herself. Or him.

He talked in a torrent then, words spewing forth in waves that turned her seasick. He was leaving, he said. His entire platoon promised to an island. The ship that would carry them across the Pacific scared him, he said. He'd always avoided Lake Michigan, the sight of so much blue. And beyond that voyage, surely filled with nausea and loose bowels, once they arrived at a speck on the map holding foreign beauty and horrors, well, what could he be but terrified?

And above all that, he said, his eyes leaking at the outer corners. He worried for her. About her. Alone, changing, unknown.

"I need you, Bev," he said, his lips trembling. "I don't care what you write about. Will you write me when I leave?"

"I will write you," Beverly said. Quinn, so alive and here. She could repeat his words back to him. It was so easy.

"Tell me anything, Bev," he said. "Just write.

Promise me?"

"I promise you," Beverly said. So easy.

He wiped at his eyes. "That's all I need to hear," he said.

She almost told him then. The space he gifted her to maneuver, to lie by omission, chafed. With a fierceness that shocked her, she wanted to tell him everything, to break him a little. Punish him for assuming the best. Teach him there were things beyond his understanding.

Beverly rose from her seat. She put her hands on his shoulders, the crisp beige of his dress shirt starched under her thumbs. She eased her legs on either side of him. He said something in surprise, but she kissed him, her tongue on his lips and in his mouth. He grew hard under her.

She pulled off her threadbare argyle sweater, her beige brassiere, and pulled her long army green skirt up.

"Open your eyes, baby."

She did.

Quinn was alive, and he was happy, and he was here. He was a husband who ate what she made him without complaint, who liked juvenile knock-knock jokes, who memorized the L train times and watched their arrivals on the platform like a giddy boy in short pants. He hated when friends would insult the Negros that sometimes pushed past the white membership rules of the union. He put a blanket over her legs when she'd spend a Saturday afternoon napping on the couch. He was a terrible liar and so refused to do it; he was a quick learner at all things with his hands and became the neighborhood handyman; he gave thoughtful gifts each Christmas, a gingham scarf she'd once admired, a silver letter opener embossed with her initials, a purple and gold vase to house the dandelions she pulled from street curbs.

He was hard muscle, instead of soft curves. But she could still let him love her.

She stood, pulled down her thin white briefs, unzipped his pants. She guided him into her as she straddled his lap. He gasped and shook, then moved, grabbing her tight against him. She took his right hand, the one he wrote with, the one he probably shot with, and guided it between her legs. She closed her eyes. She heard herself making noises, her voice trembling as her legs did, getting louder as she got closer to some goal she couldn't name, something her body knew to seek but she never had. When she found it, when his fingers under hers rubbed something loose, when she jerked and moved and cried, then laid her head on his shoulder as he did the same, her eyes squeezed shut the entire time, she thought of dirt, the shattering sound it made when shoveled onto a coffin.

Later, lying in their bed, after he kissed her again and again, told her how she surprised and delighted him, taking charge like she never had, she held his hand tight. She could feel him drifting to sleep.

"Does it feel good to shoot a gun, Quinn?"

He grunted.

"Do you think it will feel good to shoot a man?"

He lifted his head from his pillow.

"Will you be sad?"

"They're not men."

He kissed her cheek, then laid his head back down on the pillow.

When Beverly slept, she dreamed. She was a pilot in a Japanese plane, soaring above Pearl Harbor, firing on all the American ships and sailors below. She was frightened, sickened. All those tiny dots of men below her, the long ships that looked like boys' toys. Her guns sliced through them, through the water. She was powerful, and dangerous, and when she turned the stick and pushed buttons, dots ran and ships broke. Her fear and sickness went away.

Sensing her softness, or wishing for it, he pulled her into his arms, petted her. Promised that he'd be OK, that he'd come back to her.

In that place where Beverly lived now, between the known and unknown, the impossible and the real, the man she should want and the woman she did, the person she should be and the woman she was, Beverly cried, and let Quinn comfort her.

Quinn left the next morning. He thought they might be heading for Guadalcanal. He said he'd write, and he'd be home soon. Just a brief wait, he said.

But the minute he left, after the door closed and silence returned to their apartment, it was like she'd imagined him. He was an abstract creature, made of smoke and whisper. And the words of such a being, even if they spoke of real, factual, formed things like heat and guns and death, even if those words were written on paper and traveled the world to reach her, those words wouldn't be enough to grip. They couldn't steady and guide her.

So that afternoon, Beverly went back to Mary's. There was no time to wait, no time to waste.

She stood outside Mary's door and knocked. She knocked again. And again.

A figure in the window, behind the gauze curtains. A figure of curves and curls.

Beverly put her palm to the window's glass. "Let me in," she said.

"It was a mistake," Mary said from behind the glass.

"Let me in," Beverly said, louder.

"You have to go," Mary said, the voice warped by the window and something else. "Go home."

"I won't."

Mary left the glass. Her shape disappeared a moment in the house, then Beverly saw the shape return.

"Mary."

The curtain moved in and out with Mary's breath.

Beverly pressed her forehead on the glass. "Mary."

"Quinn. And Frank."

"They're gone."

"But they'll be back."

"Maybe. But what about right now?"

A stomping noise, frustrated feet on wood. "I don't know what this is."

"Does it matter?"

Beverly waited, and thought of more syllables and

sounds to make, more commands, denials, force in language. But this door wouldn't open based on such things. Words were small, insufficient. Instead she laid her body tight against the wood, knowing Mary listened on the other aside. The sounds Beverly's body made would not lie.

The door latch clicked. Beverly righted herself on shaky feet. Mary pulled the door open and stood in the frame.

"We shouldn't—"

And before Mary could say another useless word, Beverly pulled her face into her hands, and Mary gripped Beverly's shoulders, and they clung to one another with the only language that mattered.

There's all sorts of talk, Bev. The guys are thinking we might be deployed closer to the mainland. Tokyo eventually. That's all I can say without the censors cutting in. We hear we're winning, but it doesn't feel like it. The things I see every day. ~~Bodies aren't Bodies shouldn't~~ *I've never been so scared. You know how it pains me to say that?*

I won't be the same when I come home to you. And I don't know who I'm coming home to. But we'll figure it out. We have to. We'll have our family finally. We'll do everything we talked about.

I have to believe that.

At the Foster stop, in September, 1945, after it was all done, Beverly slid Quinn's letter back in its envelope.

Another uniform had come to her door in summer. The telegram a formality, since he'd been a ghost to her for years.

You don't write a ghost. Even if he doesn't know he's a ghost. You don't write an imagined and abandoned idea.

Beverly wavered once. She and Mary were reading the *Tribune* at Beverly's apartment. The painfully long list of dead. The world was building a new layer of crust, the bodies of millions seeding the ground for a darker crop.

"Do we tell them?" Beverly had asked.

"What would we say?" Mary kept her eyes on the local Chicago news in her hands.

"Don't wait for us?"

"They're not waiting for us," Mary said. "That was our job."

Beverly had newsprint on her hands. Dead names on her skin. "Maybe we tell them what a waste it would be, us waiting."

Mary put the paper down. She ran an inky hand down Beverly's hair. And Beverly remembered. Even if they were only their real selves in this bed, or in Mary's. Even if they were only this moment, or a few more, or as long as the war lasted. This, their two bodies and hearts, this was the only thing that was real.

"Silence is kinder," Mary had said, as she pulled Beverly into her arms.

At the L stop. Holding Quinn's words, written when he was still alive and harboring misplaced hope, in his generals and in her. Written when he was alive and angry.

That night, looking out her window at the cemetery, she saw them, all of them, Quinn and Mary and all the others. She saw back to that night they all smoked and drank and danced around one another, on top of the dead. She wondered if anything pure could last, if she could wait.

She saw Quinn standing in the moonlight, staring back at her.

PRETTY GIRLS MAKE GRAVES

HER

"Rosie."

In a message of static, the name was clear.

"Rosie."

Forty nine seconds the message ran on my cell. From an unknown number with a distant area code. When I first played it, on the way to the small cabin off Route 84, I was only half listening.

"Rosie."

By the third listen, I knew the speaker was male. He used a name I'd abandoned. He repeated the name five times.

"Rosie."

The static, the caller, both sounded so distant. Like they came from one of those suitcase cell phones from '80s movies. Back in time and far across the country. As I drove the mountain roads, listened to The Smiths and other music from before I was born, the message was the words of a stranger, for a stranger.

And then I was at my new home and there were things to do. So I forgot about the message. I lost myself in schedule and task, like a true soldier.

That first day, I picked up food and gas and duct tape from the bait and tackle shop down the mountain. I weeded and pruned the wild thicket of grass and bush that bordered the front path, cut back the vines that hid the front door, filled the bird feeders. I swept the bare wooden floors, dusted the cobwebbed ceiling and wood-paneled walls, wiped down the kitchen sink and tub. I oiled my rifle, stripped and reassembled it, then did it again, only slightly slower than my best time in basic training.

Done with the house, I cleaned myself with a damp towel, under my armpits, between my legs, behind my knees, where the sweat had pooled and become salt. I poured cold water over my hair, then cut it off, close to the scalp, in big black chunks that fell to the floor like fur. Then I sank deep into the cracked leather recliner, a cloud of dust rising as I fell, and put a hand on my belly.

I wanted a girl. That seemed selfish, knowing what she and I would face. Knowing it'd be easier to be a boy. But all the same, I pictured a little girl with knobby knees, braids, missing front teeth. We'd plant a garden for flowers and vegetables, get some sheep and goats, live by our own work and in our own world.

My daughter would need a name. I still had a few months to decide. But of all the things that were frightening to me about those months of preparation, and the act of pushing her out safely, and the months after, doing all I could to keep her alive, naming was terrifying. Naming a thing confers power; giving her a name could give her strength, or take it away.

Holding her, in the quiet cabin and the decaying chair, I thought of the message again.

"Rosie."

He sounded lost, lonely. A garbled distress signal, sent to a woman long turned ghost. I pitied him.

HIM

Her voice asked him to leave a message. The sound of her nearly drew blood. It sliced, a garrote to the gut. When it was his turn to speak, he lost all language. All the words, all the names for things, disappeared. Except hers. He said that name, again and again, and by saying it, he said he was coming. He told her to hang on.

HER

I dug trenches. Around the perimeter, where the wild grass gave way to trees and gravel, I dug steep drops. I went slow and easy, slipping the shovel into dirt wet from the previous night's thunderstorm, letting her move within me, giving her room to breathe as I did.

I talked to her as we worked.

"A good trench is a lost art," I told her. "We don't create lines like we used to."

When I'd talked to the cabin owner on the phone, an old woman who'd advertised on Craigslist and asked for pennies, she'd said the cabin was pre-war. I asked which war. She laughed.

"At least in the First World War," I told my daughter as we dug, "you knew which side was which. Even if they were only separated by a few yards. West trenches, the good guys. East trenches, the bad. In the middle, no man's land."

I thought of maps, systems of deep lines rutting across a continent. Like arteries, veins, things that bled deep red and smelled of rust.

A few feet down, I jumped in the hole.

"A little bit more," I told her. "Enough to crouch and give line of sight, while still protecting. Since it's just us, it doesn't have to be much wider than this."

My hands shook, and an angry red line of welts and blisters budded on my palm. Behind us, a football field away, the sun was setting behind the cabin.

Down the mountain, I heard the sound of a motor. We went to my knees in the trench, counting the seconds. One hundred and fifty one passed before a crap Hyundai with a wheezing exhaust pipe cleared. Another eighty-six before the motor faded down the other side.

"It's tight," I told her. "But it's good notice."

HIM

Everyone told him she liked cities. She'd mentioned St. Louis, Chicago, San Diego, they said. Places full of people and far from their town, which was twenty

minutes from Des Moines. But he remembered that
night, how she'd stared at the Ansel Adams on his
living room wall, the one with snowy peaks, a river
shaped like a snake, storm clouds above all. He'd asked
if she'd been to Wyoming, and she'd shaken her head
like it was heavy, like it hurt.

He'd asked questions. He wanted her to feel his
attention, his effort. See that he was worth her own.

But she'd brushed them aside. Taken off her shirt,
pants, bra, underwear, before he could swallow his swig
of Stella.

She stood naked, her brown skin straining over thin
bones, her long black hair a veil, and stared at those
mountains. Even when he'd kissed her, tasted her, slid
himself inside her, called her baby, she looked away,
into that black and white world.

HER

At night I took to sitting on the grass beyond the front
door. No lights in the cabin, or outside. Ants crawled on
my legs. Lightning bugs brushed my cheek. Owls and
bats screeched in the night wind. The light of other
worlds beyond this one shone above.

Sometimes I'd put on some music, cue up my favorite
song. Sometimes, I'd listen to the sounds of wild things.

"This is peace," I told her. It felt good to name the
feeling.

She turned, kicked. She'd started moving more
within, and I thought of alien films, the creature lurking

under skin, ready to burst forth in a shower of blood. I thought of shrapnel, alien bodies slicing from the other side to get in.

"We can't help it," I said as I spread my hands in the grass behind me. "Being around other people. We can't help fighting for what's ours."

My first week over there. My first trip anywhere, to a country I'd never wanted to visit. In the dry cool of a desert night, the girl in my platoon. The skin over her liver and pancreas a useless flap of red, her right cheek gone, gums and bloody teeth shown to the world. Her left foot hung from a shred of tissue that looked like the chicken drumsticks they fed us. And my pathetic kit: IVs, needles, cloth, tubes, shears, clear liquids. Tonics and potions. My own gun at the ready.

My girl kicked again.

"What's your name?" I wondered if there was a name that would give protection as well as power. Could I brand her, so all could see she was not to be touched? What language would that be?

I pictured her, afloat in her placenta, speaking her own aquatic language. An amniotic language, based in my body's heartbeat and rushing blood and rolling bile.

When I first got back from Iraq, I did what I was supposed to. I got a job at the pizza place in the main square. I took a couple classes at the community college in the next town. One of my teachers talked about dialects and languages, how English and Arabic and Spanish, all the world's languages, derived from the same language. Over time, people moved away from their roots, developed new words, created wholly different languages to separate us from each other.

I wondered, looking at our cabin, at the dark, at my trenches, if all those different languages came from mothers, searching for the right sounds that would mark their children as safe.

HIM

For months, he tried to figure it out. Why did she run? When he had love to give?

From his corner stool in the bar he'd seen her walk in, alone. Darkness in her hair and skin, but also under the hoods of her eyes, streaming behind her like jet contrails. Most guys wanted brightness. The cool girl, up for whatever. She wasn't like that, he could tell.

He thought of her naked beneath him, her skin dark against his gray linen sheets. There hadn't been many women. He wondered sometimes if she was even real, if he'd dreamt her. It was only one night, after all.

But he wouldn't have dreamt all the angry red marks on her forearms or how her pores smelled like grain alcohol. He wouldn't have dreamt her slack cheeks and lips when she looked at the ceiling, at the armoire, how quickly she flipped over so he couldn't see that slackness. He wouldn't have dreamt how dry she was inside, like a desert, how she insisted he push ahead anyway. He wouldn't have dreamt that she'd leave so quick, ignore his texts.

When he found out where she'd been, it all made

sense to him. She was wounded. She needed him. He'd
been waiting for someone to need him.

HER

I finally played the message again. It was a code to
break.

We drove down the mountain one day, toward the
river. The road scribbled Zs back and forth across the
hill. "Code used to be something much different," I told
my daughter. "Now it's all computers. You'll probably
learn it by the time you're a toddler. But back then, it
was math. All done in the brain."

I'd watched a movie about Alan Turing when I got
back from Iraq. He and his mathematicians and spies,
British code breakers all, cracked the German
command. But then, they let Allied ships and German
Jews die to preserve their secret and win the war.

After an hour of slowing and accelerating, curving
and straightaways, without seeing another car, we
reached an empty bank at a thin stretch of the river. I
patted myself, checking gun on hip, knife in bag, baby
in belly.

Outside the water rushed past and the air felt
thicker, heavier.

"Rosie," the voice said. Surprise and excitement.

The static could have been harmless background
noise, the chatter of a shopping mall, the echo of an
interstate, the tumult of zoo animals. It could have been
a connection over frayed wires and an aging landline.

Or it could have been a message, its emptiness full of meaning.

"Rosie." Confused. "Rosie." Anger. "Rosie." A call for shame, guilt. "Rosie." Resolve.

I listened to it again, the volume as high as it would go. The speaker didn't sound like family. The static didn't sound like this, like the mountains and wilderness.

Later, after he won the war for them, the Brits jailed and castrated Turing for loving men.

In Iraq, slicing through camouflage to repair gashes and gunshots, pushing aside the boy or girl's artillery that had failed to protect them. Each person reduced to a code, something to crack in order to fix them. Every decision I made led to death or saved a life. Things made sense.

Back home, in the bathroom of the pizza place, when I took my test and it came back positive, things made sense again, for the first time since I'd come home. I knew what to do.

I threw the phone into the river, underhand, so it skipped across the surface once before sinking.

"That's not my name," I told my daughter. "I don't think it ever was."

HIM

He talked to regretful people every day. In order to get their insurance payout, they had to go through him. He inspected their cars for damage, drank coffee in their kitchens, watched their cigarettes shake as they described near-fatal side-swipes and rollovers. They questioned their decisions, those they made consciously and those their body made by rote. For a while they would feel unsafe, jumpy, unable to make decisions. He filed his reports back in his cubicle, and they received their money, and they would feel better, and he would feel fulfilled.

After meeting her, he wished he talked to more liars. That was the domain of the freelance private investigators working for his firm. They sought out fake addresses, sorted through pain pills, interviewed exes and conspirators.

He knew a PI, a stocky Swede who he'd dealt with on a past claim. He asked the PI for a few reports, a bit of legwork, suggested it was a current case. Not fully a lie, not fully the truth.

The PI found her numbers, and the region of Wyoming she'd run off to. Specific roads to roam. Learned where she'd been, who she'd been. The PI said it wasn't a surprise, her leaving. Vets, especially medics, have their decisions made for them over there, meals, clothes, schedule. All they decide is moment to moment: how to save themselves and others in the midst of combat. Returning to normal life, choosing a fabric softener, a sandwich, a jacket for the cold, becomes incomprehensible.

He leaned on that pain. That trauma. That's why she ran away. Without her wounds, she would have seen him fully, seen what he offered the first time. Maybe they could laugh about it later, how full of regret they might have been at never getting together. Their near-miss.

That's what kept him going, through the months of unpaid leave that threatened to turn into unemployment, through the false stops and starts of his clumsy investigation, through the long hours in the ailing Hyundai that wheezed and coughed its way through the Wyoming mountains.

HER

"Rosie."

I heard his voice in my head long after I threw the phone out. Lying in the musty twin bed with daffodil sheets, the mums comforter thrown back. My daughter was taking up more space, making her presence known, and it made me hot and cranky.

"Rosie."

Not family. No trace of Mexico in the vowels, the R. I was the first and only one born here. My mother used to shake her head at my American accent, the blasphemy of contracting syllables, letters that only sounded like themselves, all in the nasally twang of rural Iowa.

With one hand I felt for the shotgun, laid out next to me like a pig-nosed scarecrow. The other I curled over her.

Her name. It had to be shield, but it also had to be code.

"They tell you," I said to her, "that you can be

anything." My hand moved across the expanse like a vacuum. "There's so much potential, and the only thing holding you back is you. It's a lie. You'll be a woman, you'll be brown. Poor. So they'll try to send you off to a war, to help you reach that potential."

I thought of my mother. She named me after a pretty, delicate piece of nature. It didn't protect me.

Did she survive my leaving? She knew what it was like to run. Without too many details, I'd heard her stories of leaving her town and country, and once here, leaving my father. She had believed the lie. She half-expected my report cards filled with As and Bs to also come with stacks of cash. She shrank two inches when the reports, my good behavior, my clean ears and clean vagina didn't come with scholarships and the keys to all the cities. Her hair started falling out in clumps when I told her I enlisted. While I was gone she got lost at grocery stores, found herself driving with no memory of where. When I got back, she found my bed empty again and again, found me harder, absent, unfamiliar. If you're not better than me, she'd said, what was it all for?

"I'll try not to live through you," I said to my stomach. "I can't promise I won't live for you."

Out here, maybe the rules would be different. Maybe we could truly be who we were meant to be.

. . .

HIM

He drove the same roads, the same Zs, up and down. He waited for the laws of attraction to guide him. He was losing his hold on the things that used to guide him: facts and figures, reality and truisms. He was losing his hold on her dark eyes and smooth shoulders.

Driving, foot on the brake of the downward slide, foot to the gas on the climb.

He was wondering if this had been a mistake, if she was too far gone to be saved.

He was veering into doubt, unsure if she was worthy.

He was worried he'd imagined a future that wasn't there.

He was scared he wasn't the man he thought he was.

And while he was drifting and worrying, on a partly cloudy morning with the chill of fall descending, on a steep grade, his motor chugging and something else ticking, he saw a flash of white as it fell into and under the ground.

He pumped the brakes and eased onto a gravel path he'd missed before. He scanned the grounds, saw a tiny cabin tucked far back from the road, and a deep line of ditch between them.

HER

It took me longer than it should have to recognize the sound of the motor. I held my daughter and my rifle as I raced across the field and jumped into my trench.

Too late, though. The motor cut. The car door creaked. The boots crunched.

No one knew I was here except the landlady. She said she'd never visit, leaving me to my business. But maybe she changed her mind. Maybe it was a nobody with a flat tire. Maybe it was something else I hadn't accounted for.

"No trespassing." My head still below the dirt line.

The crunch of gravel stopped for a moment. The wild world was silent, as if even the birds and insects sensed the invasion.

"I have live ammo," I said. Louder than the last warning.

"Rosie?" The gravel again, ground under someone's shoes.

I stood, my torso above the trench, and aimed the shotgun.

HIM

She had an impossibly long gun. Her hair was chopped, leaving uneven patches of white scalp. Her breasts hung loose and low under a white t-shirt. But it was her.

He'd imagined how it would feel when she finally saw him. He'd imagined it, here in the wild, as the secret relief of being found, a smile that would slowly win out over shock or fear.

She saw him now. Really saw him. And being seen was terrifying.

"Who are you?"

"Rosie," he said. The man was early 30s, white, with ash-blonde hair. He had the advantage of height, six feet to my five-and-a-half, but beyond that he was thin and lanky. Not much to him.

"Who are you?" I said it a little louder this time.

"Rosie," he said. "It's me." He pointed to himself, in the direction of his chest. Like his whole self was tied up in his heart. The gravel announced his next step. He should have pointed to his throat, his voice, the one from the message.

"Who are you?"

"Rosie please, it's me."

"Stop," I said. My weapon was well-oiled, well-kept.

His face seemed to seize, his lips and jaw and eyes working through too many emotions to settle on one. "Don't you remember? It's Paul. From that night?"

A liar gives too many details, confidently. He was vague, rattled. "Whoever you're looking for, she's not here."

"You look different," he said, gesturing to my hair. "But I'd know you anywhere, Rosie."

"That's not my name."

"It's the name you gave me," he said.

I looked him over again. Flattened nose, thin lips. Long earlobes. Rough patches on his arms near the wrist, maybe psoriasis.

There'd been so many, in those first months home.

My fingers, instead of tying off veins, inserting IVs, handling weapons, were arranging cheese and ham slices on pizza crusts. My feet, instead of sprinting across hard-packed dirt and aged stone, sat still under a school desk. My back, instead of carrying half my weight in gear, guns, supplies, spasmed at night from the weight of nothing. My body was purposeless, foreign. I thought someone else could make me feel it again. I'd go into bars already drunk on cheap vodka, pick someone with thick arms or thighs, a tight ass. Sometimes they just needed to meet my eyes and not falter under naked need. I left each of them before the sun came up, before they could try again.

A vague memory of his shape, moving between me and a black and white image of mountains.

"If we had a night," I said. "That was it. Go home." My voice was not gentle. I had my gun.

HIM

It was all going wrong.

"No," he said, shaking his head. Throat closing around tears. "Not without you! I came to help you. Bring you back. Or go somewhere else."

She wasn't putting the gun down. She wasn't melting in relief. She wasn't telling the truth.

If he could just hold her hand, look into her eyes. Skip the words. She was looking at him now, really looking. She would see the two of them, as he did.

Gravel squeaked as his boots left the path for the grass.

"Stop," she said again.

He was close enough now to see more of the ditch in which she stood. It was freshly dug, without grass cover.

"What are you doing, Rosie?"

"I'm telling you to leave, and never come back."

HER

The man looked so hopeful. He'd found me, when I'd worked hard not to be found. Under that white skin with angry red patches, the smile he was working hard to keep, the blonde hair that stood on end in the wind, revealing a bald patch, something desperate thrummed.

But I was ready. I felt my spine straighten, my grip tighten.

When I learned about my daughter, I knew she could be from any of the men, all of them. Even this man in front of me. But she belonged to no one but me.

"One more time," I said. "Leave now."

HIM

"But," he said. From his place in the grass he could see more of her now. Her slashed hair, chunks of scalp, pert ears, long neck. Her feet were bare in the dirt. Her white t-shirt, wet under her arms and long, past her knees. Her shape, under the shirt.

He stared hard at that shape, matching it to his memory of her body, and finding something new.

All the reasons he'd considered for why she ran, all of them had been about hurt and fear. All of them fixable.

He hadn't considered this. Her shape, sudden and unmistakable. And as he worked through the math, added up her belly, her flight, their night together, did the sums and multiplied by new layers of shame, trauma, a mother's ferocity...

He smiled. Laughed. It was wonderful, this new discovery. Full of promise. Potential.

"Our baby," he said. He held his arms out wide.

When the blast hit his chest, he thought his heart had exploded from joy.

HER

The shot sent birds flying and rabbits running. All the creatures that had welcomed us, let us pretend to be wild, one of them, were now wary.

I held the gun up for another five minutes, watching the body, counting off the seconds.

When he didn't move, I leaned back against my trench wall. I gripped the dirt with my bare toes. I flexed and curled, flexed and curled. Breathed.

After more quiet seconds, that shape was still there, still immobile. I patted myself down, patted her.

"We'll move on," I said.

I felt her deliver a tiny kick under my belly button. Then her foot slid from my skin, back into her amniotic sea, where the sound of my heart and blood slowing lulled her to sleep.

"Lots of wilderness out here."

The rest of the afternoon and night I'd bury him in the trench and backfill the rest. Drive his car down the mountain and set it on fire. Pick up our things from the cabin and lock it tight. Start again.

I hummed to my baby as I got to work.

DIG ME OUT

A FEW WEEKS BEFORE THE MUSIC STARTED, I CAUGHT NINA
out back, stomping on light bulbs with her pointed
kitten heels. She had a package of brand new halogens
and was pulling them out one by one, hurling them to
the pavement with a fierce overhand, then stomping on
the fragments. I hung back between the dumpster and
the door, fully aware I was acting the creeper. But I'd
never seen Nina break. She was peach lip gloss on
brown lips, smoothed bun at her nape, crisp linen blazer
over scalloped sheath. Poise on the skylit showroom
floor, our best salesperson.

But here she was behind the store, alone. Grunting,
almost growling. The sky was darkening into another
early April storm, and she cheered when thunder finally
broke.

I watched, all slack-jawed and idiotic.

*

I don't know if something switched off all of a sudden,
or if she lost her words one by one and we just didn't
notice. But I do know she sold even better while silent.

Her first customer was in the Shia Collection, LivingLand's basic couches, made of a *microfiber blend.* Jonas and I called it the Shit Collection, made of *the fuck is this?* material that got pregnant with dander and skin cells after each sitting.

The barely-adult woman saw Nina coming and her freckled shoulders seized up around her tiny white ears. This type of girl would always say she wanted minimal, simple, easy to clean. Code for cheap. We're supposed to talk about quality, longevity, our new 2017 financing that lets her afford what she really can't, and then we're supposed to guide her towards the Movanta Collection, all suede and leather.

But instead of the standard spiel, Nina just smiled.

Between her front teeth she had a gap just wide enough to catch your eye, and one incisor presented at a slight angle. On her lips she wore coral or sienna when she wasn't wearing peach, and against her black skin the color shone and hid at the same time. Under her bottom lip was a pucker, not quite a dimple and not quite a cleft.

Nina's smile was something, and it worked on the girl in the Shia Collection that day. You could watch as her instinct kicked in, the girl instinct to fill the quiet — first with a laugh, a short *ha* of surprise or nervousness or both. Nina just kept smiling, the sunlight hitting her crooked tooth. The girl looked around for help or translation, but she didn't spot me and Jonas watching from a few aisles back, beyond the

TV stands. Saliva glistened in the corners of Nina's smile.

I was going to intervene. If it were Garry or Larry, our skinny lifers with gray nose hair and gray skin, both of whom relied on Republican-grandfather disapproval as their sales weapon, I wouldn't bother. And I definitely wouldn't bother with Harry, who prays over his snacks in the breakroom, his black hair parted severely down the middle and his voice all off-key octaves, like he's just hit puberty again.

I took a few clicking steps across the showroom floor, in my heels that pinched and rubbed my left big toe. But I stopped when I saw that the girl was leaking globs of black mascara down her cheeks.

"I know," she said to Nina. "I should … But it seems so pointless."

Nina still smiled, her lips closing over her teeth now. Her hair was half kink and half curl, and today it wasn't in the slicked-back bun. It was wild, circling her head like storm clouds.

The girl was crying harder and shaking too. Jonas and I mirrored lit eyes and crooked Os.

Nina placed a hand on the girl's shoulder.

"Never enough," the girl said.

Nina patted, then pointed her toward the back door.

They were gone a good ten minutes. Jonas and I traded theories on what this new ploy was, wondered why Nina would mess with her already stellar sales record to try something new. I remembered the light bulbs, but I didn't tell Jonas.

When they returned, the girl was almost skipping. Tears gone, a brightness in her eyes and cheeks, hands and jeans dusty. Mute as a mannequin, Nina guided her to the register and through the financing application process for a $5,000 leather sectional.

Once the girl was gone, we crowded Nina.

"Ballsy as fuck," Jonas said. "Did you know she was going to cry?" He touched Nina with the tips of his fingers, like he expected some sort of electric current. I touched her too, my palm on her forearm, because the situation seemed to allow it. These were signs of our curiosity, and I think it showed some admirable restraint that we waited a good twenty seconds in silence for Nina to talk. When she didn't, Jonas cracked first.

"You want to keep your secrets, I get it," he said. He rolled his eyes my way as he left.

Annoyance flared in the back of my neck. Somehow my emotions were all tied up at the top of my spine, near my throat. The surge was starting, the messy mix of lust and frustration and confusion, my brain filling with constellations. Finally Nina broke.

"Everything I say comes back to me one day. Everything you do comes back to stare at you."

Her voice was a yowl and yodel at once. I heard guitars and drums too, heard them so clearly I looked around the store half-expecting to see that some stray musicians had set up shop. The air vibrated like the speaker reverb at a Wooly's show. My ears were ringing before I realized she was gone.

*

That same day, LivingLand attracted a lesbian couple
wearing duct tape on the soles of their oxfords,
matching arm tattoos, and carrying the weekend's
circular, folded to the *Bargain Buys* page. Nina led them
out the back door. When the couple returned they were
holding hands and brandishing the pickup ticket for a
full-price bedroom set. In came a single mom with twin
girls in tow, her eyes sunken with deep dark bags,
utility bills at the ready to prove her new address. She
asked for a foldout futon. Nina gave her a smile, then
gave the kids Tootsie Roll Pops before leading the mom
outside. Twenty minutes later, the stock crew was
helping the mom load princess-themed bunk beds into
her rusted Windstar.

The others peppered Nina with commentary. Larry
and Garry joked about "black girl magic," which, as
Jonas said with a cringe, at least indicated they had a
tiny, tattered bit of wokeness. Harry said something
about the sin of pride while looking at Nina's breasts.

I watched Nina, and considered how little I knew
her. In another place, another year, I would have tried
harder to connect. Maybe I hadn't because of Bruce. Or
because of the humiliating layoff from my account exec
role, and the shitty job market that had landed me here
a few months before. Or because I was always tired and
irritable, my feet aching every day in unsteady heels.
Nina was: thirties, single, no kids. That's all I knew. She
never mentioned family, or whether she'd grown up

here in Des Moines, or whether she'd had a career before LivingLand, like me.

I made it to 4:45 before realizing we'd skipped lunch, all of us. It was the time of day my slacks started to chafe at my waist and my buttondown tugged at my bra line and my toes hurt, the time of day I cracked and re-cracked my knuckles, slapped my cheeks, shook out my arms. The time of day my neck ached the most.

At six, I slipped out the rear door. There were just dumpsters back there and the loading bay for the delivery trucks. A new layer of broken glass blanketed the pavement — light bulbs and jars and blenders.

I jumped as a new bulb sailed down and shattered at my feet.

"*You got your words,*" Nina sang, against a guitar's off-key wail, a military drum. "*But they make you stuck.*"

My mouth moved, trying to match hers.

*

I saw Bruce that night. In the living room of my one-bedroom ranch off Fleur, we sat drinking vodka sodas and PBR among the Movanta pieces I'd purchased in flusher times. Bruce painted houses by day, and at night he'd try abstract stuff. Wiry blonde hair framed his face, grooming subservient to art. There was black in the beds of his fingernails.

He'd told me on our first night, after we'd matched on an app, that as a kid he'd never liked coloring books — all the lines and rules. We were at the Alpine, and he also told me, over bottles of Blonde Fatale, that falling for a woman was like falling for a song. He put a finger on the back of my hand. He said men are drawn in by the shape of a song, just like the shape of a woman. You listen to it, you get to know it, it gets in your head, and it goes around and around.

He used that moment to kiss me, breath hot with chicken fingers and hops. I closed my eyes and thought about the brevity of songs.

That first night in my queen sized Tempurpedic, fucking me from behind, he asked what I'd do if a girl was with us, so I knew he wanted stories of my crazy, lecherous bisexuality. I painted the image I'd used with other guys of his type, stolen direct from a porn clip of two girls sucking the same dick.

We'd been seeing each other a few times a week, for a few months. In my living room on the night of Nina's singing, Bruce told me again that he loved me. So formal, like a royal decree: "June Kullen, I love you." I sat very still, on the same principle as an animal camouflaged in plain sight. I'd so far dodged the need to respond.

I thought about broken glass, storm clouds, hair circling around her head like a tornado.

I'd waited for someone to treat me well, never sure if I was waiting for a man or a woman. I'd known, ever since my career had nosedived off a cliff, that finding someone good would give my life meaning, a way to show I was a success.

Distracting Bruce was easy: I climbed into his lap.

After sex, before falling asleep, in that weird space of nothing and everything, my mind flitted through images of customers, fabric samples, memes, thoughts of bodiless sex, fingers in holes, anxious headlines and the daily bout of nauseous fear, Beth Ditto lyrics, St. Vincent lyrics, the Yeah Yeah Yeahs.

And then I was up, on my phone, riding the comet trail of a memory into Google.

*

"She was singing," I told Jonas as we walked across the LivingLand parking lot the next morning. "Sleater-Kinney songs." He usually wore solid grays and blues, but today it was a brown striped shirt with red chinos. He walked faster than normal.

"Should that mean something to me?"

"Nina. When you weren't there. She sang to me." We were the same height, and usually the same pace. But today I skipped to keep up.

"June, you're obsessing like a hetero dude."

On normal mornings, and during normal lunches, and over normal happy hours, we'd talk sexual escapades, embarrassing drunk texts, our favorite episodes of *Riverdale*. We were cubicle mates at our last job, had been laid off together, sent each other Bonnie and Clyde gifs. Jonas was funny and fun, always insisting we go out for birthdays and meeting-someone-new days. But whenever I thought about who I'd call in an emergency, Jonas was not it.

"She sang. But not really singing. First time, it was 'Don't You Think You Wanna.' I knew it sounded familiar. Then 'Things You Say.'"

He stopped, and I stepped on his camel-colored brogues.

"Why are you dressed up?" I asked.

"And what are you wearing?"

I looked over his head as he opened my jacket to see the flowing, bell-sleeved peasant blouse and A-line skirt. Probably the most feminine thing I'd worn since eighth grade, when mom and dad insisted on a white dress for church photos. I'd flipped off the photographer mid-shot, leading to an epic grounding but no more fashion requirements.

"You think you're going to whisper *Sleater-Kinney* and Nina's gonna go lez for you?"

I buttoned my coat and left the Nina story unfinished. Jonas kicked at the broken glass outside the back door, grumbled something about animals digging in the trash. I didn't say anything.

The entire sales staff came to work ready to experiment that day, emboldened by Nina's new methods. Larry and Garry were a tag team, modeling their approach on odd-couple sitcoms and buddy-cop movies. One would play the soft, the good listener who's just looking out for the customer's happiness, and the other would play the hard, the voice of reason and right and easy credit at rapacious rates. But neither of them seemed eager or able to play the good cop. Larry tried offering an ear and shoulder to the frazzled mom with Irish twin toddlers, but his disdain for snot made him break character. Garry's fear of fag behavior meant he couldn't relax a muscle while trying to empathize with the bearded guy in Carhartts and sweat-stained Iowa hat.

Harry brought a Bible out on the floor, and the customers parted before him like the Red Sea, or ran headlong in the opposite direction.

Jonas went full homo, hips cocked, tongue between teeth, vamping his way towards suburban moms longing for their own personal gay. He took long breaths full of dramatic tension, allowed pregnant pauses after they spoke, liberally used the lingo he'd previously outlawed in his vicinity: fierce, sashay, honey, AF.

From the main desk, I watched them all moving through their new acts like dying circus animals.

"Smile pretty, take take the money."

Nina stood next to me, and when her wail was done and the guitars gone, the chorus rang in my head. *I'm your little mouth, did ya want me?* I opened my own mouth, just to see if Corin Tucker's voice would come out. Nina watched me in my muteness. I tugged at the silky bells of my sleeves, patted the back of my head where my dirt-colored hair formed a V. For the first time in decades, or maybe ever, I wished I had longer hair, something to cover my neck and drape my shoulders.

"At least they're entertaining, even if they're not going to beat your record."

She cocked her head, eyebrows raised, a challenging look.

"Nah," I said. "I've sold enough for the month."

As we stood watching, I tried to remember things Nina had said in previous lunches and work breaks. Did she speak much before all this, or had Jonas and I talked over her?

"Does it make you angry, the guys trying to beat you?"

She shook her head, which counted as talking in my mind.

I wanted to ask her what had happened, but didn't trust my memory anymore. That heat again, in the back of my neck. I cracked my knuckles.

"Does breaking all that stuff out back—"

"I'm a bubble in a sound wave, a sonic push for energy, exploding like the sun, a flash of clean light hope."

She was very close, our chests near touching, and then there was music in my head, direct through my ears into my brain, into my spine. It felt like "One Beat" had been written for her, and for me. I heard it, but also felt it, felt the heavy pound of Janet Weiss' drumsticks on that canvas in my breasts, felt in my throat and crotch the stairstep jump and climb and fall of Corin Tucker and Carrie Brownstein's guitars, felt in my bowels and knees Corin's corralled bay and howl.

"Your word for me is fusion, but is real change an illusion."

My teeth ground and eyes popped and hamstrings shook. Me, at my own private concert, speakers and woofers aimed at my heart. In my head I saw crazy things: me in Nina's bed at the mercy of her tongue, me in space above the earth, me in shock therapy biting down on brown plastic, me in Harry's hell that looked like Mordor, me punching kicking screaming at men in suits, at men on apps, at men in alleys.

When she stopped singing, I wobbled and tripped, grabbing onto the faux-wood desk.

*

I went home and watched live sets by the band on YouTube. There was shitty footage of shows back in '95, emerging from the ashes of the Riot Grrrl scene, full of discord and agony. Higher quality clips emerged around the millennium, when they experimented with melody, and even had a peppy and poppy video for "You're No Rock and Roll Fun." Then the mid-aughts sets saturated with the end times, as they became virtuoso rock gods only to call it quits. Tight, masterful reunion shows from 2016, boosted by Carrie's new fame on *Portlandia*.

I'd heard about the band as a teen because Corin and Carrie dated. Male rock critics seized on that, even outed them to their families. At the time, knowing I liked boys but also girls, I wished I could be outed by somebody else, just to avoid the task of a one-on-one with my parents. And I wished I had someone to make things with, like they did, even if my own experiments with guitar playing resulted in pleas for mercy from our neighbors.

I put my fingers to my throat, probing. Like it was a soundboard, full of dials and levers. Like I could amp up the vocals, access that nodule of anger and hope and love and fear that the band turned musical.

*

The rest of the week the men's new tactics brought them middling success. Nina took every woman out back, and sold her something big and moneyed after.

She remained mute for them too, the LivingLand guys, and they seemed to like her more for it. I heard Garry tell Nina about his oldest son's meth problems, heard Larry tell Nina about his oldest *daughter's* meth problems. Harry told Nina about his congregation's black member, how well he spoke and snappy he dressed, how Harry sure found himself thinking about the man a lot.

Even Jonas. I came back from a bathroom break one morning to find him scrolling through Grindr with Nina at his arm, showing her each option before swiping left or right.

"But he's so pretty," Jonas said when she swiped left on a shirtless trainer. "June! Nina's helping me look past the pubic V. She's gonna find me love."

"Since when do you want love?"

"Jesus take the wheel," he said. Harry trotted up and gave Jonas a lingering high five.

I watched these guys with Nina, little babies all.
Come inside, I am the shelter.

The top of my spine itched, and my throat ached.

*

Bruce stayed over that Friday night, and in the morning, after spooning slipped into sex, he asked what we were doing the rest of the day. We were lying on our backs, and I felt him looking at me while I looked at the ceiling. I told him I needed to run some errands. He offered to join me, and I said no thanks. He stared at me in silence, and I stared at the smooth white paint.

"Why don't you love me?"

"I didn't say that."

"I'm doing everything right. I don't hurt you, I treat you kind."

"You do."

My throat ached again. I could hear Carrie's words. *My baby loves me, I'm so hungry. Hunger makes me a modern girl.*

"You want a girl, don't you. You're really a lesbian."

"Bruce."

"My friends told me bi doesn't last. Just a phase to going full dyke."

"Don't use that word."

"It's just a word. I'm the most feminist guy there is."

"Love is just a word."

"Cunt."

He got up from the bed, stepped into his pants with

quick, jerky moves, threw on his hoodie. Looked back at me, where I still lay naked — my small breasts, my full bush, my knobby limbs, my short hair. He shook his head.

"Look at you. You're like a boy."

"That makes you gay."

He yelled more *dykes* and *cunts* and a few *bitches* as he tore through the bedroom and living room, a full Sherman's march on his way out of my house.

My baby loves me, I'm so angry. Anger makes me a modern girl.

*

I found myself driving to Nina's place, half expecting her to greet me, to know I was coming, to know better than I could why I was there.

Nina had a Beaverdale brick, the type of house known for dark wood molding, claustrophobic stairwells, chimney and wood fireplace. I'd found the address on our staff contact list.

On her step I realized how invasive this was. But I pushed the bell anyway, and Nina came to the door in blue track pants and a white sweatshirt.

"Will you talk to me?"

Nina smiled.

Inside, I took in the blue walls, abstract prints, mid-century brown furniture, before bubbling over.

"I know I'm imagining what I was hearing. So could you talk to me?"

Nina's smile curved a little, crumbled a little.

"Stop fucking around!"

She opened her mouth, and I felt my diaphragm clench up. Then guitars, Corin's "whoo whoo" and Carrie's voice, *"I've got this curse on my tongue, all I taste is the rust, this decay in my blood."*

I flopped down on the sofa, the cushion firm but yielding. The song was "Sympathy."

Nina went into her kitchen, and I blinked a few times. Her house was bright, nearly ultraviolet with the sunlight streaming through her south-facing windows. I heard water running and cups jostling, and pictured some movie scene, where the hostage taker comes in on false pretense, planning his attack while the host and hostess cater to her.

One living room wall was covered in crates stacked on their wood slat sides. Records filled some, X-Ray Spex and Pixies, Nina Simone and Arcade Fire, Rachmaninoff and Michael Jackson. Books filled others, by Lorde and Baldwin and Murakami. The prints on the other walls all featured reds and burnt oranges, isosceles triangles and rhombuses.

I felt better. Like I was making an effort, understanding her more.

Nina came in carrying two mugs of coffee with spoons and a couple packets of stevia. Her hair was tied back with a yellow scarf, and she smelled like anxious armpit sweat.

"I'm sorry," I said, taking a mug. "The last thing you need is a reminder of work on your day off."

"Ready to find fragments of stillness." She dug in her pocket, pulled out a light bulb. One of the old ones, nice and round and inefficient. I took it, and laughed a little.

We stirred our coffee, the spoons scraping the bottom in a way that rang like a siren.

"My boyfriend left today," I said. "Sort of boyfriend. I guess I sort of pushed him out."

Nina watched me, and I watched the shadows of some outside tree branches moving across her Berber carpet.

"I should be happy with him."

Nina opened her mouth.

"I feel like I should be able to breathe if I have what I'm supposed to."

"All your life is written for you." The syllables of "Call the Doctor" were piercing.

"Yeah," I said. "Do you think anyone knows what they're doing? Really?"

"They want to socialize you, they want to purify you."

"It's like everyone just plays at being adult. Grabs on to these guideposts in the distance as the way to go, and judges everyone whose grip isn't so tight."

"I'm no monster, I'm just like you."

We sat for a moment, my neck firing, jaw clenching, knee rabbiting up and down. I guess she must have felt it, because Nina put out her hand, hovering over my thigh. She had stubby fingers, bony knuckles, long nails but torn cuticles. I willed her to move her hand from its spot of comfort and calm, lower to something else. But it stayed in flight.

"I wish I could do whatever you're doing," I said. "Singing, or channeling, or whatever. Does it feel like you're, I don't know, being yourself?"

Nina looked away, to the walls and her paintings. That's when I knew I was using her. I knew it. And I also knew that she might be speaking in plain English.

Maybe I was imagining this music. Maybe it was really me slowly breaking down into sounds and snippets. And she was clearly telling me to get some help.

My knee slowed, and my stomach spun.

Maybe I was creating my own Nina, replacing her in her body, crafting a mute, all-knowing good witch. A being that served me and my story.

I stared hard at the records, willing the letters I couldn't quite see to form into the words I wanted. A Sleater-Kinney album here would be proof. It would show I wasn't dreaming while awake, that I wasn't developing some sort of schizophrenia. Especially a clueless white variant, with hallucinations based on stalkerish lady lust and magical-negro stereotypes.

The moment stretched and thinned and nearly snapped. I knew I should go.

But I looked back at Nina. And I thought I could see the girl inside her, under that skin, the wild and loud and brash thing that was truly her. The one that was singing to me.

I didn't care if I was sick, or breaking. I thought about how Nina might be able to see the girl under my skin, if she wanted to.

Speaking was so small. So I leaned forward, whispered *"you've got the darkest eyes,"* diminished and poor without the music behind "One More Hour," but still better than what I could say on my own. I kissed her.

She pulled back, and this time her smile was full of pardon and reprieve.

I watched the carpet shadows again. The silence was huge, but not big enough to disappear into. The back of my neck scorched, and I squeezed my hands into fists.

We were both buried in these bodies, and I thought about how good it might feel to lash out. Since words didn't help, what if we broke some shit, beat somebody up. Smashed this light bulb. Got a gun.

But since I only dressed sort of boyish, and remained firmly woman, I just slunk out of the house with a mumbled apology. In my car, the steering wheel got my half-hearted punch. I jammed my thumb in the process.

*

I spent the night listening to all the albums, back to back, again and again. Maybe I hadn't listened enough, or listened *closely* enough. I pumped up my phone volume until the sound was a tinny rattle. Then I put in earbuds, lay back on my dirty sheets, clicked the volume up again until the music felt like a vise, squeezing and pushing its way in.

When my eyes started watering, the ceiling plaster whirling and melting, I hit pause. The silence felt expectant, moist with possibility.

I opened my mouth and waited for the music to come.

When it didn't, when my throat produced only a shaky exhale, I put my earbuds back in. I swallowed four Advil.

Carrie sang me to sleep: *"I'm tired of waiting on a ship that won't leave shore, the water's bloody with the ones who came before…"*

*

That Monday morning when I stepped out to my car, the air was oppressive, thickening as I breathed it on the drive, swamp-like when I got out at LivingLand. I avoided Nina all day. Avoided Jonas too. I sat behind the main desk looking at pictures of the band on my phone.

The day turned to afternoon, and a hot wall of muck made its way into the store, carried on the sweaty shoulders of customers.

"The fuck? It's April, not August," Jonas said. I ignored him, and he rolled his eyes. "What's with you now?"

A clap of thunder made us jump. We looked outside to the parking lot, where rain was pummeling the pavement, whirling loose deli wrappers and sandwich foil like tumbleweeds. Larry and Garry had their hands and noses on the glass, and a shock of lightning lit them like x-rays.

"Tornados can't come this early, right?" Jonas said.

And as if he called it forth, the east side siren began its drone.

Harry sprang into action, hands on hips like a comic boy scout. "Storeroom, everyone!" He was already shepherding a pair of Latina women, our only remaining shoppers, toward the back.

"What about those two assholes?" Jonas said, pointing out Larry and Garry, the gray men who now suddenly seemed to be shot through with color as they stood at the front doors looking out, clapping along with each peal.

Nina was behind them one moment, but next we knew she'd pushed through the double doors and out into the rain. Now the siren was screeching up and down in its Doppler effect.

Larry and Garry yelled at Nina to come back, she'd catch her death, but she kept walking out toward the edge, away from the line of cars, nearly to the street, her face up to the rain. Harry screamed at us to get moving, get inside, get to the storeroom safely away from the windows. But I could see Nina out there, raising her hands above her head, water pouring over her shoulders and arms. Jonas squealed as another firebolt lit the bruised sky, and the power went out in the showroom, and the streetlights went out in a cascade of sparks.

Then the rain stopped. The sky turned purplish-yellow and the wind calmed and all went silent. Those of us who grew up in this city, in this state, in this region, knew what came next, even if we'd never seen it ourselves.

I saw Nina's pointed finger first, and then I and Jonas and Larry and Garry and Harry, all ignoring the rules we knew about basements and windowless rooms and how to ride out these storms, we looked to where Nina pointed. The funnel was less than a mile away, twirling as it descended. We watched it make landfall, and then the sound hit us: the metallic screeching, creaking of wood, and a wailing, like nothing human, like old steam trains barreling along their tracks. The tornado lifted off the ground a moment, then plopped down once more, a giant vacuum tube sucking up pieces of earth and house siding and trees.

It screamed so loud I felt like it came from inside me.

We watched as the funnel took a sharp turn, a diagonal line headed our way.

The men were all action, running towards the back, shouting at me to follow.

Outside stood Nina, the funnel a football field away. Her lips were moving, her throat contorting, but I could tell she wasn't afraid. She looked like she was singing.

The door in front of me rattled, and for a moment swung open, a foot's width of access to the outside, and I heard the siren, the shriek of the tornado, and maybe, a snippet of a song. I followed it, pushing the door wide. I kicked off my heels and ran. I cleared the building and then the wind knocked me off my feet, but I got back up, my left palm bloody and dotted with asphalt grit. I was running for Nina, my bare feet slick as roller skates, my gait lopsided as a drunk. She saw me coming and closed her mouth, smiling small. She shook her head a little and drops of water flew off her hair.

I opened my mouth — to say I don't know what. But we were shocked into a crouch, the sound of ripping behind us. The funnel had reached the corner of LivingLand. I grabbed Nina's hand and she gripped mine as we watched the roof peel back, revealing wood, girders, concrete and wires.

"It's like skin," Nina said, her voice high and loud. But there was no music behind it, no lilt and wail. I wondered if I'd imagined it, her speaking, and I looked at her, hair blown above her head, eyes wide and white. I gripped her hand tighter, afraid she might chase after the storm.

I felt tight in my throat, like I'd swallowed a square ice cube whole, a triangular nacho, a rectangular cracker. Edges fighting their way out.

Skin, I thought, as the funnel seemed to slow, the corner of the LivingLand roof curling like the top off a cat food can, frozen at a moment of equilibrium breached, any more peeled and the whole thing would go.

Nina's eyes on me, her fingers squeezing blood from my palm.

Out of my body, out of my skin, I thought.

My throat tight, bursting, my cheeks puffed, my breath held, I opened my mouth.

Acknowledgments

Thank you to M. Allen Cunningham, my friend, mentor, and editor, for believing in me and in this book.

Thank you to the mentors who provided essential guidance as I wrote this book: Karan Mahajan, Robert Antoni, Keija Parsinnen, and Alison Wellford. Thank you to my MFA peers, who read and improved portions of this book: Margaret Montet, Jessica Klimesh, Pearl Griffin, Rachel Caruso-Bryant, David Roth, and Erin Snedeker.

Thank you to Annie Hwang, for your guidance, your validation, and your graciousness.

Thank you to the magazines, organizations, and editors who shared early versions of stories from this book with their readers: *Atlas and Alice, Epiphany, Foglifter, Reader Berlin,* and *Barrelhouse.*

Thank you to the Atelier26 Books team, including Nathan Shields for his gorgeous cover design.

Thank you to the incredible authors who read this book and offered their generous praise: Carter Sickels, Melissa Faliveno, Jeannie Vanasco, Karan Mahajan, Chanelle Benz, and Robert Antoni.

Thank you to the city of Chicago, for thirteen years of incredible highs and devastating lows, all of which informed this book. Thank you to the city of Des

Moines, for raising me, for testing me, for welcoming me back.

Thank you to my family of friends who have supported me, traveled with me, and kept me laughing while writing this book. I hope this makes me even more witchy in your eyes.

Thank you to Erin, my Broads and Books podcast partner, for weekly joy that sustained me during literary ups and downs. And for greeting every piece of book news with excessive exclamation points.

Thank you to Elaine Hoversten, who asked me what I really wanted to do, and who I wanted to be.

Thank you to the musicians who inspired and informed the stories in this book: Nancy Sinatra, Nine Inch Nails, X-Ray Spex, The Pixies, Bikini Kill, Future Wife, Sonic Youth, Arcade Fire, The Smiths, and so many more. And special thank you to Carrie Brownstein, Corin Tucker, and Janet Weiss. For Sleater-Kinney, for "Dig Me Out," for giving sound to our rage, and for making beauty ugly and ugliness beauty.

Thank you to the (many, many) agents and editors who rejected my first three never-to-be-published books. You were right: they weren't ready. I hadn't lived enough, I hadn't written enough. You made me work harder, learn more, and take risks. You helped me get here.

And thank you, reader. To be able to write that is the gift I've always wanted.

PERPETUA'S KIN *by M. Allen Cunningham*
An enthralling multi-generational mystery, reworking of Shakespeare's *Hamlet*, and profoundly contemporary exploration of the American experience as embodied in one family shaped as much by tumultuous world events as by each of its members' long-kept secrets. "Gorgeous. Devastating. Lyrical. Addictive." —Powell's Books Staff Pick Fiction/Literature/ 9780997652376

A THOUSAND DISTANT RADIOS
by Woody Skinner
Longlisted for the PEN/Bingham Prize for Debut Fiction
Written with dark humor and folkloric flair, Skinner's stories capture the passions and compulsions of modern America in unforgettable imagery and saturated color. Skewed, hyperbolical, sometimes surreal, here is fiction honed to cut through the blur of our times. "Skinner has some keen and lethal potential. There will be blood." —Philip Martin, *Arkansas Democrat-Gazette* Fiction/Literature/ 9780989302395

PEOPLE LIKE YOU *by Margaret Malone*
*Winner of the Balcones Fiction Prize / A Powell's Books "25 Books to Read Before You Die" Selection *
From the Finalist citation for the PEN/Hemingway Award: "With great delicacy and wit, the nine stories in *People Like You* constantly beguile and surprise. In their matter-of-fact humor, which is often laugh-out-loud funny, they tap a long tradition of American humorists. What sets them apart are Malone's protagonists: dark, troubled women unafraid to puncture the pieties or to confront the void." Fiction/ Literature/9780989302364

FUNNY-ASS THOREAU
with an introduction by M. Allen Cunningham
The so-called hermit of Walden Pond was constantly tossing off jokes, whipping out witticisms, and making fun of himself and others. Here, in the first collection of its kind, is Henry in his own words as he tries to wrangle a pig, pees in the woods, loses a tooth, elaborates on his dislike of other men's bowels, and more. "Hilariously irreverent."—*Thoreau Society Bulletin* Nonfiction/Literature/Humor/ 9780989302388

BIRD BOOK *by Sidney Wade*
An exquisite array of sublime and playful poems dedicated to the wonders of winged creatures. Poetry/Literature/ 9780997652338

THE HONORABLE OBSCURITY HANDBOOK
by M. Allen Cunningham
Offering solidarity to any writer or artist working against the grain of the times. "Ingenious. Important, wholly absorbing, inspiring and inspiriting." —CYNTHIA OZICK Nonfiction/Literature/Essays 9780989302302

See all our titles at ATELIER26BOOKS.COM
and subscribe to our podcasts on your app of choice:

IN THE ATELIER, *a creativity podcast*
exploring the life of the imagination, and the
highs and lows of making art

THOREAU'S LEAVES: *the Thoreau Podcast*
an atmospheric immersion into the world
and work of one of America's greatest writers